The Field Where All The Flowers Grow

For my mum and dad who always make sure I know how loved I am, and for everybody who taught me the importance of kindness, perseverance, and strength.

Email – felicityemmagraceotoole@gmail.com

Instagram - @felicity_jayne

Prologue -

She's a home-made birthday cake with pure white frosting and rainbow sprinkles. She's the smell of rain blessing the burning pavements in unbearable summer heat. She's the non-silent silence that follows you through a walk in the woods. Unexplainably peaceful. Of course, before I knew what I know now... what you're about to find out... I had no response to the question, "Who is Maria?" I dread to think what they would've thought if I had looked them right in the eyes as mine bled out with love and said, "She's the smell of cool rain on a burning sidewalk." So I'd smile back with a warm heart and say, "She's my mama's friend."

My mum, Mary Elizabeth Pinnock, died when I was three. The only memories I have of her are the silly little crayon drawings I drew of her at kindergarten. Golden hair. Bright blue eyes. But, I mean, they may not be the most reliable pieces of evidence, because I don't imagine she had three arms, or a skirt made out of sunflowers, or a rainbow for a smile, like she did in some of my masterpieces. I could never ask my dad about her. He re-married when I was seven and threw out all real pictures of her as soon as the funeral was over. The only real connection I had to her was Maria. Her best friend. She lived in Texas (where I spent my childhood before moving to the English countryside) and earned her living as an artist - painting, modelling, and crafting special gifts. As a child, I would receive monthly letters from Maria, in a cream envelope, sealed with a stamp of lavender wax and a deep royal purple ribbon. I would write her back and include polaroid pictures of what I was up to, using my stepmother's old camera. I'd savour them in a pile under my bed and read them whenever I was hurt inside. The pages, christened with her delicate handwriting, thrived with kind, wise, and comforting advice.

Dad isn't her biggest fan. In fact, as I've grown up, I've noticed how twitchy he gets when her letters arrive. He always sorts through them and hands them to me, almost strangely saddened by the clear, kind intention behind each word. The sound of the letterbox, always accompanied by a louder, eyeroll. "The woman reeks of the smell of grief. I want to move onwards, not backwards, and she makes me think of your Mama, Journey.

Don't talk too much about her. Especially not to me." He would warn, whenever I opened my mouth to gloat about Maria's existence. The more the need to do so was oppressed, the more I found myself thinking of her constantly, and wishing with my whole being, that she was right there with me. But she wasn't ever.

Until she was.

Chapter 1 -

Smoke. Throat scratching, nose tickling smoke. "What the *hell* have you done, woman?" My father hurtled his voice at my stepmother, Rosie. I sat up immediately and headed downstairs to find her flustering over a tray of black, crumbling strips of extremely burnt bacon. An eye-stinging veil of smoke filled every inch of the room. "I'm sorry! I'm sorry!" She cried huge tears of redemption, but my father had slammed the front door, forcing the whole building to shake. I had no idea where he was going, they had to leave for the airport at lunchtime. My 'parents' were going on one of their quarterly vacations without me. I actually, thinking back on it, had no idea where they were even planning to go. Only that they would be back in two-ish weeks, and I was under strict instruction to keep the house spotless.

Out of clear frustration, Rosie threw her blue, rose patterned oven gloves to the floor, and stamped on them as if they were on fire and she was trying to extinguish the flames. "What did they ever do to you?" I asked jokingly, trying to make light of the situation. I never truly loved the woman, but I hated my father far more. Rosie snapped, but she never exploded like he did. I never had to take cover or hide from her. In fact, when my father dramatically decided to refuse me dinner without a motive, she would sneak me little napkins full of food and swear me to secrecy. Even still, Jordan Hunt was a scary man, but I never really thought him capable of more than vile insults, the occasional shoe throwing, and outbursts of explicit rage. Not then, anyway.

 "You're not funny. Sense the tone." Rosie snarled, smashing a glass accidentally and then kneeling in the pile of shards and weeping bitterly to herself. The crumbs of massacred tumbler sprawled effortlessly around her in a peculiar, almost staged formation. "Let me clean this mess for you. You'll get all cut up," I offered, helping her up. She had saddened denim coloured eyes and bright blonde hair. When standing, she snatched her arm back and composed herself, straightening her skirt and apron before leaving the room without another word.

Reluctantly, I ran a sink of hot, sudsy water and plunged the crusty, greasy tray within it, scrubbing at it with a scouring pad until at last, the beige foam turned to white soap, and I could run the tap and the water would run clear. Every few seconds, the streaming tear of water would crack and spit viciously at me, spraying the countertop and floor, dampening my sleeves. Once I had dried it up, I put it away and swept up the glass before brewing a cup of tea and taking it to Rosie. I folded the sleeves of my yellow silk button-down, over my hands, so the cup wasn't so hot, and then walked anxiously up the stairs to deliver what I hoped would act as a relaxant. I hoped wrong, apparently.

"Rosie?" I called serenely into her bedroom. "I cleaned up the messes and made you a drink." The door was left open a crack, so I nudged it with my shoulder and saw through the gap, my stepmother, staring out of the large arch window, looking out across the fields. From here they looked like a toy farm play set with tiny, fake, movable fences and farm animals that were created from little hard bits of plastic. "Leave it on the table." She sighed shakily, gesturing loosely but not turning around at all. I heard the door open and we automatically both flinched, bracing for the stinging sound of my father's gravelly voice. But, as soon as I heard two sets of footsteps I knew they were far too cushioned and light to be my father's. It was Darcy. My father's much younger sister, and my absolute muse. "Don't worry. It's just Darcy." I reassured Rosie, closing the door and turning to see my beloved best friend at the top of the staircase.

As I looked into her big, brown eyes, I was certain that Darcy was the most beautiful lady in the world. Her hair was made up of soft, silky curls, and enriched with a deep, dark, almond tone that flickered red, honeyed as tree resin when exposed to sunlight. Despite being my paternal Auntie, Darcy and I were often mistaken for sisters. My father and Darcy were the only two blood relatives I had ever known. She was my absolute world, and I adored every second I spent with her. She grinned wide and lifted me off the floor, squeezing me tight and burying her face into my wavy hair. She wore this olive green summer dress with puffy sleeves, and some brown boots. "Oh! you're almost taller than me!" She exclaimed, setting me down and moving my hair to behind my shoulders. "One of us had to reach a reasonable hight." I mocked, fiddling with a shiny badge on her tassel rimmed leather jacket. "Where did this one come from?" I asked, noticing it was new compared to all the other pins which I had seen a million times. She collected them from all over the world and every single pin had a marvellous story behind it. "A sweet boy named Lucas brought it back from New York for me!" She twirled around, showing off. "Where's your Dad?" She froze, noticing the silence of the house. "Rosie burnt breakfast and he got really mad and stormed out." I whispered, nearing her as if she were a shield from all the bad in the world. "Hey, don't worry. It'll just be me and you in a little while. Are you hungry? You wanna go out and catch a bite to eat? We don't have to wait for them to go, you know," She said, confidently. "You don't think he'll be mad?"

"Not at you." I looked thoughtfully at the door and re-entered it cautiously. "What do you want now?" Rosie sliced, defensively.
"We're going out. I won't see you now until you get back. I hope you have a lovely time." The sad, small mess of a woman half smiled. Smears of mascara cupped her tear brimmed eyes like dead, upside down crescent moons, leaking grey blood onto her pale cheeks. "Yeah. Bye."

Darcy took me outside to her forest-green pickup truck that gleamed and twinkled in the shimmering sun. "I have the perfect spot for lunch." She whispered, playfully. I giggled as she grabbed my arm and ran to the car. "Where? Where are we going?" I squealed, as she tickled me and threw me in the passenger seat. "You'll have to wait and see, my dear." She revved the engine, and we soared off into the day. Darcy drove us down all the familiar roads until none of them were recognisable, and we were heaving the breathless truck up an enormous, grassy hill. "Your Mama used to make picnics all the time. Almost every week, we would go to this beautiful field, with all these-" She stopped suddenly as if she had cussed. "All of these what?" She pretended not to hear me. "Darcy?"

"Oh, I forgot what I was saying. Oh, the picnics. Your Mum. Yeah." She trailed off and spaced out for a moment until at last we reached the very top of the monstrous hill. Around us, there were barely any signs of civilisation, accept a few barns and ranches plopped here and there. Buttercups and those tiny violet flowers, the name of which I cannot seem to remember, swayed happily in the slight but present breeze, which kissed the world around me.

In the back of the truck, Darcy had adorably set up a picnic like the ones she had begun to tell me my mother had introduced her to. A gingham, pastel green and cream coloured blanket lined the surface, so we had protection from the chilling, naked metal. She excitedly opened the door up, and we sat in the open, snacking delightfully on lemon bars, candyfloss grapes, berries, and tortilla wraps, until our hearts were content. I traced invisible heart shapes on the blanket beneath me, with my finger. "Do you think they're gone now?" I asked feebly, remembering the existence of my father and his almost always artificial wife. The berry on my tongue turned sour, and I had to try really hard to swallow it as my stomach tensed, and I felt as if I could feel the food digesting within me. Almost as if she hadn't heard me again, Darcy looked out across the land as if she were in another, far, far away. "Darcy?" She flinched and stammered clumsily which struck me, because she only ever did so when drunk, and in that moment, she hadn't a drop of alcohol in her body. "I- I- don't know." The way she looked at me churned my stomach and I felt my lips tingle the way they do when you panic quietly to yourself. Her eyes spilled with obvious despair, over what, I didn't know, but I could tell I had something to do with it. "Why are you looking at me like I only have five minutes to live?" I asked, laughing nervously. Without a beat, she gave a huge, choked sob, and laughed all at once, but then the laugh faded, and she just let out little, breathless cries of lost hope. "I'm sorry. I'm sorry. I am just really proud of who you have grown up to be and I know your Mama would agree with me completely." I wasn't at all convinced that was why she was crying but played the part, telling her thank you, hugging her and making out shapes in the clouds until she suggested we drive back to the house.

The Field Where All The Flowers Grow

As the car jolted and jerked down our front pathway I closed my eyes and clenched my fists, my nails denting the palms of my hands, stingingly. I seemed to believe that if I wished hard enough, my father and Rosie would have left, and I wouldn't have to be swept into the pitiful aftermath of their morning spat. It worked... Well truthfully, the fact I wished for them to leave probably had less to do with it than the fact they would've missed their flight if they hadn't. Darcy dropped me at the porch and spun around, insisting on buying takeout for dinner as a treat to make up for her out of character and emotional blabbering.

As I re-entered the place I had been trained to call home, I was overcome with memories so strong they felt the way it feels when you bite into a lemon or take a spoonful of bitter medicine, only the feeling was in my heart, not my mouth.

I laid silently on the sofa for a while, reminiscing about the times my dad had been a good Father. I had to think of them now, in order to revive them and protect them from extinction. There weren't ever many, but now they were so scarce it was sickening. I could feel my heartbeat speeding up as I grew increasingly irritated. My blood began to burn and itch within my veins and tears prickled my eyes with cruel intent. Just as I thought my heart couldn't grow any faster... The letter box clanked, and my heart fluttered when I saw a cream envelope sealed with a lavender stamp and royal purple ribbon, tucked peacefully upon the ironic 'welcome to our happy home' rug, that hugged the front door. The house felt like it was full of people I loved. The sky looked brighter. I felt present. I traced the edges of the envelope with my finger and felt my heart slow to a tranquil tempo. My blood no longer scathed, and my tears no longer felt like thorns. Without any hesitation, I carefully opened the envelope and slid the paper out from within it, smoothing the pages with my hands. The pages spoke gently of a place I hadn't visited since forever ago - though I still ached for as if it were home - and old stories of my Mother and how she painted my room three different colours the week I was born for fear I didn't like the first two. I really loved Maria, though often she felt like a daydream. A distant but present memory. The feeling you get when you're trying to remember something, before it comes rushing back to you with a satisfying magnetic force. I sat, reading her letter, and imagining how her voice sounded, while cuddled in the corner of the sofa, submerged in a loose, thin, and cool blanket. The smell of burning meat soon faded with every gracious word I read, until at last, the room smelt of rose petals and safe.

When Darcy returned, she seemed like a different person. Her usual buzzing, dancing, lively self. When the sun had gone down, I took myself up to my room and laid cosily in my bed while holding Maria's letter in a hug. When I was very little, I wrote to her about the bad dreams I had, and she told me if I put her letters under my pillow, or under my bed, they would ward off any monsters of nightmares with their magical powers. When I grew older I learned that she only made that up to comfort me, but I still never slept a night without them under my bed. They remained there always, and I loved every speck of their existence. The way the paper felt. The way I wore the ribbons in my hair. The way the pages smelled.

In the middle of the night, my door creaked open, and Darcy snuck inside, laying on top of my bedcovers and holding my hand distantly, as if I were a child crying in a storm that she resented for interrupting her sleep. As if I had called out for her to come quickly, in a pained voice. The sky was darker that night than I had ever seen it before. Blacker and deeper than you can imagine. And there wasn't a single star in sight. It rained heavily for hours, forcing branches to knock intrusively on the windows, so hard I assumed they would break at any moment. I dreamed so many times that the window truly cracked, that it became an impossible task to tell when I was actually asleep and when I was just dreaming. But through both, consciousness and unconsciousness, the wind whistled a daunting tune accompanied by a single other instrument. Darcy's empty cries.

"I can't do it! I won't do it, Jordan! I don't care! No! NO!" I sat bolt upright and clutched the duvet tightly in both hands mercilessly, without a care of how it may leave them creased and wrinkled with frustration. Had he returned? "I'LL HANG UP!" No. Phew. I leapt from my bed and practically jumped down the entire staircase in two strides, to find Darcy vibrating in insufferable anger. "Okay, okay. I'm sorry. I'm sorry. Forgive me, please, oh God, forgive me." She sobbed into the phone with everything she had, and then saw me and immediately stopped. Not because she wasn't upset anymore. More because I had shocked her into knowing she had to stop. The phone was hung up and set down, and then, as the blinds behind her danced solemnly, washed in a glossy, gold air, Darcy smiled. "What did he say?" I asked, my throat dry.

"We're having a grown up spat, no need to worry, my dear." I followed her protectively into the kitchen where she reached for a bottle of red wine.

"Tell me more. I'm old enough to know. I want to know." I whined, leaning over her, and taking notes on her every move, as if I could use them to create a formula that could make me be just like her. Graceful, rough around the edges, confident, keen, curious, and kind. "I'll tell you what, you run and find me a bottle opener, and I will tell you everything you wanna know. Okay?" Her voice quivered. It had never done that before. I halted but she blinked quickly and gestured towards the door. I headed straight for my father's office.

The interior to that room was ambient compared to the rest of the house. Leatherbound books with earthy coloured covers lined the shelved walls, and lamps hung from a copper bar in the centre of the ceiling. Candles dreuled wax into puddles on rough, chipped wooden desk surfaces, and a locked safe, the home to Dad's bottle opener (or church key as he would frequently call it,) sat solidly by the jarred window. The window actually never closed properly, so a damp, mould stain that looked like the marks of fierce talons, trickled down the wall underneath the windowsill. I knew the code to the safe, but not the reason it existed.

 I wish I had held onto that last little flurry of innocence left in my soul before I opened up that big brassy box. One outreach of my hand, and everything was about to change. Thinking back to it makes me feel nauseous.

I reached down, into the safe's guts and produced out, a soft blue book, cushioned and bound with a thick leather strip. I scarcely looked at it, and thrust my other hand back into the safe, feeling the cold, slick walls for a sign of the opener, when suddenly I spotted it, sticking out of the book I was holding. I relieved it of its position, plunged within the pages, and accidently caught glimpse of the contents. It was a diary. My mama's diary.

September 15th, 2004

Your Dad did a superhero thing Today, sweet girl. He got his two-week chip. I'll explain what that means when you're a little older. I can't wait to look back on this time, when we're past the bumps in the road, and feel overcome with gratitude that we got through it. For you. Auntie Maria baked me the most delicious muffins with fresh, strawberry jam she made herself. I hope she'll teach you how to bake too, one day.

September 16th 2004

Your Dad had a little set back Today, but he's strong enough to fight this, and I'm so very happy to help him do just that. I will wait patiently for the day in which I hold you close, as it is getting me through these hard days. I hope you always know how much of a blessing you are to me. To us. You are already so loved, and you aren't even here yet!

September 17th 2004

You're here! Early, but so precious. I'm in love with you already. I will keep you safe always.

December 10th 2007

Hi, Baby. I used this book to document my pregnancy with you, when you were just a little bump. I haven't written here since, but in case I never see you again, I find comfort in knowing you may find this when you're grown. I know your Dad is planning on taking you far away tonight, because he is having a little trouble again, and I think he is unnecessarily worried I will try and take you from him. I tried to fight for you, but it will be bad for us both if I follow. I trust he will bring you back to me when he has calmed. But in case such a thing never happens, know I will always be your Mama, and I will always love you more than any words can express. I will be okay. Maria is here with me, and she and I will wait for you, forever. We will be together again one day. I know it.

The Field Where All The Flowers Grow

I dropped the book on the floor and sat on the hard wooden chair behind me. Darcy appeared at the door. "Journey, how long does it take to-" She stalled, dead in her tracks and for a moment, shuffled uncomfortably back and forth, her mouth glitching and spluttering until at last she said, "Where'd you find that?" She sunk to the floor as if she longed for it to swallow her whole. I couldn't move. I was quite literally stunned. "My mum. Isn't dead? She didn't die? My dad... Kidnapped me?" I sniffed, swaying in my seat. "M- Maria knows where my mum is. It says in the diary that she would wait with her forever." I stood up, suddenly. "Why would she- why would you- why is everybody lying?" My heart pounded and I started struggling to even inhale air. My hands began to cramp with pins and needles as if I had sat on them for a very long time. Sure, I had panicked before but never, ever once like this. This was the sort of intense panic that you maybe suffer once in your entire life. The panic that comes when everything you've ever known turns out to be the tip of a very dangerous, unexplored iceberg. Impulse started taking over like an infection – I could feel it plastering itself to the wall of every cell in my body. There was no stopping it. Whatever I was about to do, I was about to do now. "What are you doing?" Darcy stared motionlessly out the jarred window. "My dad is gone for two weeks, right?" She took several moments to process my question and then nodded once, very slowly, without blinking. "I'm going to visit Maria and find out what I can. He won't know I'm gone. I'll be back in time before he notices. And then we can decide what to do." I said, trying to gaslight myself into thinking this was a sane and reasonable, safe idea. I knew Maria's address from the letters. All I had to do was jump on a plane and fly halfway across the universe. Unsure on Darcy's involvement in the matter, I disregarded her briefly and walked into the living room.

I took a look around the pretty, little light filled room I stood in. The walls and floors and ceilings and sofas and tables and placemats and fireplaces stared back at me. They had witnessed us smile, cry, laugh, dance. Yet I was sure, if they could talk, that long history would melt away, and they would all jump at the opportunity to rat me out to my awful Father and his silly little wife. I focused in on a picture of them both and was overcome

The Field Where All The Flowers Grow

with a pang of upmost distress, when I realised
the frame used to carry a picture of my father and
I, back when I was blinded by childhood
innocence, and didn't remember knowing the
man he could become when something failed to
go his way. I picked it up and tossed it at the wall.
The wallpaper split like skin when sliced with a
knife, and a little thrashing of dust settled down
on the polished floors. Glass sprayed towards me,
but still, I didn't move. I must have stayed there
in complete and utter rage for several minutes.
Darcy circled me, talking hurriedly, but I
couldn't hear a word she said. I could see her
mouth moving but felt like the wire in my brain
that connects vision and sound had snagged,
temporarily. It was the kind of mad that makes
you feel as if all of your eternal organs are
rejecting each other just for the sake of expressing
hate. The kind that makes you blush and shiver
all at once. I could feel the fading shadows of our
past scuttle around me. So many versions of me,
had died here. So many versions of *us,* had died
here.

The clock called out to me, and I suddenly came
back to earth. I had to go. Soon. I ignored

Darcy's adamant yelling, packed a rough suitcase with clothes and bare necessities and found my passport. It was then it truly sunk in. I ran to the bathroom and threw up violently. My mum was alive. My mum was alive. My mum was alive, and she still had close contact with Maria. Who I was about to get on a plane to see. As for my dad... let us just say that I wished for some pretty unholy things to happen to him, on the drive to the airport. In the thirty seconds it took me to read the diary, and the thirty seconds it took me to re-read it to ensure my eyes were not deceiving me with a cruel façade, I had pretty much disregarded him as my father. I was incapable, at the time, of processing the idea that any right-minded human could lie to anybody they loved for fourteen years. My fears had been confirmed. He had completely fallen out of love with me.

But it was okay. I still had a Mum. She was out there. She was somebody. Somebody, I hoped, who would help me with my homework. Teach me how to cook. Tell me stories of her childhood when the world seemed like a different place. My thoughts carried me away. And in that moment. I was somebody's daughter again. Truly. I was held.

Chapter 2 –

I stayed deathly silent on the way to the airport. I told Darcy if she didn't drive me, I would walk, so teary eyed, she bundled me into the passenger seat of her car. Her usually vibrant face looked grey, and she was covered in a shine of sweat and peculiar, unexplained guilt. I was sure if my dad knew that I knew, what I knew, he would snap. And as somebody who had witnessed him snapping one to many times, I had learned the hard way that it was to be avoided at all costs. This train of thought made me see why Darcy looked so shaken. If Jordan had threatened my mother into a fear so strong she never found herself able to try and rescue me from his icy grip, I could only imagine how Darcy were feeling. If he were to find out, all hell would break loose. "I'll be back. In time. I promise. He won't even know I'm gone." I choked, looking over at her as she parked.

"I did a bad thing. I'm so sorry, darling." She

trembled, pulling into the parking space.
"You know how he gets. You don't say no to your
Dad." She sighed, scraping her hair back into a
ponytail and pulling out her phone. "You wanna
catch flight 629. Okay? Then switch to flight 28
and you'll land in Dallas. If so much as a puddle
gets in your way, you call me, and I'll help you
sort it out. However big. However small. When
you get to Dallas, you wanna get a taxi to the
address. It's gonna cost a lot but my credit card
doesn't have a limit, and we can sort that out
later." She laughed nervously, and then got out of
the car, moving around to open my door. She
handed me the plastic card. I hauled my case
down and then stepped out into the refreshingly,
damp breeze. She didn't look like Darcy
anymore. She looked sick and scared and frail
and small. I hugged her and knew I'd have to be
the first to let go; though that didn't make it any
easier. I'm glad I held onto her warm, cosy grip
for as long as I did.

It was a good last hug.

"I'll see you really soon." I breathed, holding my
bags. "See you soon sweetheart." She got into the
car, and I turned to walk away. Towards hope.

The Field Where All The Flowers Grow

"JOURNEY!" I looked back to see her hysterically crying. The sight frightened me. "You know I'd never hurt you, baby. I'd never mean to hurt you, okay?" I nodded, and blew her a kiss, and then watched her drive away, trying to be strong on the outside so she didn't see through to the lost child I felt like in my heart.

That would be the last time I ever saw her. There was no show stopping, flashback montage of our best memories. Nothing. Just a blown kiss, a wave goodbye. As if the red rose worthy show of a friendship we had held for the last lifetime wasn't worthy of a grand finale of any sort. A wisp of her fiery hair in the wind and the spotlights were blacked out. The curtain closed, never to be opened again.

I think the adrenaline of the news, clouded the next two hours because I couldn't tell you much about them. I do, however, remember boarding the plane and everything after in gritty, sharp, polished detail that I couldn't forget if I tried. The plane seats were oddly comfortable. I was never invited to the luxury vacations my father and Rosie galloped off to every once in a while.

I'd spend those weeks alone. I could cook my own food and stay up as late as I wanted. Bliss.

The little window to my right, could've been mistaken for a screen playing one of those hypnotically, gorgeous nature videos. As the people, then the trees, then the buildings and the towns were washed away by our startling height, we were thrust into the sky. It was my honest, deepest pleasure to witness that day take its final breath, among the clouds. The sun sprawling, melting, sloshing into the deep and burning red like melting butter. The vermillion then faded into a pretty pink, like the kind you might find in the icing on a strawberry doughnut, or a generic pink felt tip. Ordinarily comforting and sweet as powdered sugar. Soon, the moon came to life, washing the sunset away with a silver shadow, and casting a navy, grey, spell on the heavens. Stars began to seep through the shimmering veil of clouds like pin pricks in a masterful tapestry, when held up to a light. Accept it was alive. I felt the moonlight in my blood. The stars twinkle and shine in my heartbeat. The endless void of sullied royal blue encased my soul. It held my hand. It waited for me to fall asleep.

The Field Where All The Flowers Grow

About four hours into that flight, I was gently awoken by the lady sitting beside me, who up until now, had remained a side profile, and somebody who would remain in my story, for that flight only. An extra. A background feature. The muffled "Excuse me mam-" in the background. But instead, she chose to wake me. "Excuse me, hey." She whispered. I opened my eyes and looked up at her face. She had dark hazel eyes, caramel hair styled in very tight ringlets, and rosy lips. "Sorry, it's just... are you alone? You look very young. I have a sister about your age, and I'd be terrified if she was flying alone." Her accent was smooth and Texan. I smiled briefly. My mama probably sounded just like her. "I'm meeting my friend in Texas." I said tiredly. "But thank you for your concern." She tilted her head and giggled. I'm against judging people when you first meet them, but I really didn't like this woman for a single wretched minute I spent under her gaze. "You getting on flight 27?" She asked, intrusively. Everything I had ever been taught about stranger danger flew out of the window. "Yes. Are you?" She reached for her phone distractedly, and smiled as if she had just remembered the name of a face only she could picture. I began to feel uneasy and excused myself to the bathroom. What was I supposed to say? She would've tormented me had I refused to answer, I knew she would. I didn't have a choice and as far as I'm aware, going back and lying wouldn't have changed a thing at all.

I stood in the tiny cubicle with both palms flat against either wall. The plane air was stuffy and thick and began blocking my ability to breathe. I was forced to take jagged gasps of air to avoid suffocating entirely. Somebody knocked, heavily. With no idea if I had been in there for one minute or ten, I quickly slipped back through the door. Hundreds of eyes looked over me. I tried to convince myself that there was nothing to be afraid of, as I walked gingerly back to my seat. The woman smiled, smugly. "We're almost landing." She said, scrunching her face up and bringing her shoulders up towards her ears in a sickly-sweet manner. Her pupils expanded every time she looked at me, studying me closely as if I were an animal she thought to be extinct, until she saw it behind glass for the first time. She looked at me like I was the only thing in the world. "Cool." I sighed, nervously and held my phone tight. I told myself over and over that I probably just reminded her of her little sister. Outside of the window, I saw the world looking real again. Buildings and trees and bushes and people and grass. Smack. We hit the pavement. There was a collective cheer from an irritatingly perfect family, in the row behind us.

After entering the airport, I sped up and lost the woman, to my greatest relief. Colour saturated the picture again, and I steadied myself on my newly found suitcase as a spell of dizziness cast over me. I reached for my phone and switched off airplane mode, looking around me, still feeling like I was being hunted down. She had the hair of a golden retriever, maybe she could smell my fear like they could too. Maybe she was behind me right now. Softly, stepping towards me like a predator until she was close enough to lurch onto me and rip shreds of me apart like I was a tiny, helpless animal. Prey. And nothing more. Nope. She was gone. I found my gate and sat cosily in the caffe nearby. I tossed a little cinnamon onto my hot chocolate and sat alone in the far corner, pulling my sleeves over my hands so they didn't burn, as I brung the smooth blue mug to my lips. A flicker of Darcy threatened to come out in me, when a breath takingly beautiful, slightly older boy sat opposite me, across the room. His eyes looked kind and told a story. Of what, I didn't know, but I bet it was a good one. He suddenly looked up at me and smiled. He had dimples and soft kissable lips. I smiled back, and quickly looked away, noticing my mouth had been slightly open when he had caught me staring. For that split second, I had slightly forgotten the reason I was even in the airport. The sense of adventure and determination was turning to anxiety in my mind. What if she doesn't know Maria anymore? What if Maria was mad at me for coming without warning? I prayed that she would let the fact this was emergent cloud the fact this was an invasive, untimely, and unorganised visit.

I awaited in the airport for the next three or so hours, watching the planes land and lift off. It became very apparent to me, that I was becoming part of a hundred different people's stories. I was an extra in the background as a military Dad came home and surprised his daughter. I was a one liner 'excuse me,' as I witnessed a newly engaged couple have their first fight. I calmed my reaction concerning my own plotline, by noticing everyone had their own one. And in that moment, nobody felt like a stranger. I had seen into the hearts of about two hundred people all at once, as I waited in line to board that plane. The pretty lady in the yellow dress, the little boy twins walking their plastic dinosaurs up the rail of the stairs, the businessman who had missed his flight the night before. All different journeys flourished around me. I even noted some down on the complimentary leaflet using a biro that had been left on my seat.

Oh, how I loved to write. I was certain fate had left that pen there as I crammed words between the already existing safety instructions. Good thing I didn't have to use them, because they were Smothered in love, mystery, and thriller by the time I was finished. Writing gave me control. I could rewrite and revisit and unwrite anything at any time. I decided. I got to call the shots.

But you can't do that in real life. You can't unwrite the past. But sometimes, if you're really lucky, and really strong... You can change the future.

By Felicity Jayne

"Excuse me... Sorry... Hi. Hey. My name is Helen. From the last flight?" I looked up from my leaflet and saw the woman from before, stood right beside me. Suddenly, I was more winded than the time I had fallen out of my best friend's treehouse. "Where are you heading? I just... Figured maybe we could share a cab? My treat. If we're going the same way. What do you say?" She asked. She carried with her, an offensive confidence that quietly infected the air around her, until every atom around me became hers. I felt like I belonged to her in a strange, possessive nature, in which I would be forced to do what she said without argument, for fear of getting hurt. "A little ranch in a small town named Springston. I doubt you know it but thank you for the-" She cut me off. "Springston? That's exactly where I'm heading. I don't mean to scare you, it's just... I would be grateful if someone helped my sister out." She smiled a smile that dripped with authority and passive kindness. "I'm not scared. Thank you." I smiled, trying to conceal my nervousness. "I'll wait for you right outside the gate." And she was gone. I sunk down into my seat with a sigh and closed my eyes. The world around me seemed to dim a little, and I debated trying to outrun her, though something told me I wouldn't be able to.

When we landed, I immediately messaged Darcy to tell her, and then waited by the gate. Sure enough, the woman came and found me. Her soft features were deceiving. There was nothing soft about the person she was inside. I didn't have to get to know her to see that. "I found your bags!" She exclaimed, thrusting them towards me. I hesitated and stepped back. "How did you know they were mine?" I bit, growing more anxious by the minute. My palms started to sweat, and I was held in a frosty grip that forced me to tremble, despite the weather being warmer than it almost ever was back in England. In fact, the sun here shone so brightly I almost hated how clearly I could see everything. She stepped forward, unshaken. "I saw you carry them in." She didn't blink or flinch or miss a beat. She just stared – waiting for me to smile politely, nod and follow her. I'm not sure if this story would've ended differently had I ran away from her. But one thing I've learned, is that dreaming of a different ending can be dangerous. To be thankful for everything you have around you is far safer.

By Felicity Jayne

Because before you blink... it can all be taken away.

Helen took my arm and marched me briskly from the airport without another word. She didn't speak until we were under the harsh gaze of the sun. "Ah, I can see our car from here! Hurry now, I can't be late, you know!" She scoffed, as if I was holding her back. I fumbled for my bags and panted alongside her, for her single stride seem to cost me four of my own, despite her being significantly shorter. The car we halted at was a slick, black sports car that had no resemblance to any sort of public taxi I had seen back in England, furthering my desire to question who this Helen lady really was. But I had a strange sort of guilted trust in her. Like I owed it to her to believe she had a good motive. The driver, a solemn and secretive looking man in his late seventies, silently began hauling our bags into the boot. Helen opened the back door and ushered me inside, the sound of her shiny, black stiletto's like violent knocking at a weak, wooden door that was about to give in. The car was stuffy and hot, and the leather seats latched themselves to every part of me that touched them. The driver

The Field Where All The Flowers Grow

returned to the wheel, and Helen planted herself beside me, oddly, in the middle seat, as opposed to the left window one, anyone else would've sat in. The car started, abruptly. "Where is the address of the place you're heading sweetie?" She asked, her voice glistening with a sickly honied tone. "Posy ranch avenue." I breathed.
"Posy ranch avenue!" She called to the driver, turning to me, and smiling with a smile so big, it looked like the corners of her mouth might tear a little. I smiled back warmly, and placed my head down on the headrest, closing my eyes and pretending to sleep for the hour or so it took us to drive. The same hour it took me to realise I had done a very stupid thing.

The unexplainable luck and relief I felt as the car stopped, and Helen let me go with a dauntingly simple, "Have a good trip, it was very sweet to meet you my dear," distracted me from realising what I had stepped out onto. I felt harsh rocky terrain under me, as I plucked my bags from the boot, and had to shield my eyes as dust from the taxi's exit, polluted the airspace around me. I took a deep breath in as the brown clouds distinguished in the breeze. A gorgeous house with a wrap around porch stood alone, cuddled among fields that popped and exploded with colour. Upon that porch sat a woman. And that woman, was Maria.

Chapter 3 –

I stood very still for a moment, fearing any sort of movement I made would disturb the fresh, floral scented air, or make a sound provoking her to turn and see me. I watched her as she watched the car drive away into the distance, and waited until the groan of its engine, faded into nothing. Behind me, the dirt road carried on for as far as I could see. The fields around me stretched for miles. Some empty, some home to animals grazing thoughtfully, and some occupying woodland. Only one however, flourished with flowers. Bluebells, lavender, roses, tulips, pink and white bonnets, lilies, primroses, and dandelions danced in unison, rippling and parting in the wind as if an angel had softly reached down from her palace in the sky, and ran her fingers through the meadow with a maternal, grace. The sky was a creamy pale blue and the golden beams from the world above shone upon this scene with pride. It was the most beautiful thing I had ever seen in my life. I walked along the jagged gravel, and felt it grow finer and smoother beneath me, until I stood about seventy feet from the house.

It stretched up tall, like it was attempting to touch the heavens. The walls were white, and honeysuckle grew up the sides. The wrap around porch was made with birch wood and carved in it, were symmetrical, perfect images of trees and flowers like the ones encasing me in this bliss. I could have died right there and then, and left this earth with immeasurable pleasure, knowing the last thing I saw was that strikingly gorgeous.

I neared Maria now, with no idea of how to make myself known. Then, before I could stop myself, I called out her name. She stood immediately but did not face me. Her hands were clasped with tension, as if my voice was one she had been waiting to hear, for forever. She wore a pretty, blue dress and an apron, her light hair tied in a majestically messy bun, and ears bearing hoops that shone in the glittering sunlight. When she turned finally, her face displayed the most stunning smile, and her ocean eyes glistered with all things joyful. I walked faster now, and she came towards me, steadying her excited self with the banister beside her. As soon as we reached close enough to stretch our arms out and hold each other's hands, we did so. Maria lifted me from the ground and then set me down, hugging me so tightly it almost threatened to hurt. But it didn't. And I wouldn't have cared a bit if it had. She desperately held fistfuls of my curls in her hands, then placed her face close to mine, with her hands on my back. "What are you doing here? Oh my goodness, am I dreaming?" She asked, pulling away so she could look at me, but not letting go.

In her arms, I knew she would never let anything harm me. Even a ladybug, dare not flap her wings and waft a tiny breeze, causing a single hair on my head to move out of place. She had me. Maria electrified me and moved me the way a perfectly sad movie ending does. For a short while, we just looked into each other's eyes and wondered with a tender curiosity, if the other were feeling the same.

"I found this." I said, suddenly remembering the reason for my visit and opening my case. I was so caught up in this fairy tale moment that I had forgotten how to think. At last, my hand grazed the diary, and I pulled it out. The smile was swept from her face in the next hush of wind, and she took a step back. "Maria... I want you to help me find my mum." I said, shakily.

"Who-" She stammered, "Who was that lady in the car?" She looked around, wincing slightly as if she was scared Helen would drive back. "I met her on the plane. She said she would drive me to you. I couldn't say no. She was kind of terrifying." I sighed, opening up the diary and reading out the entry that acted as the catalyst for my visit. "Maria is here with me, and she and I will wait for you forever. We will be together again one day. I know it." I then shifted my vision back to her shocked face. "Will you help me find out what happened?" I breathed.

"Yes." She spoke suddenly without a flicker of doubt. "Yes. Let's go inside... Where is your Dad?"

"On another stupid holiday." I said, rolling my eyes as she helped me up. Maria smiled, laughing a little to herself. Her voice worked like a spell, casting me into relaxation with its calm, loving tone. In the five minutes I had spent with this woman, I had felt safer than I had in my entire life, with anybody else. Even Darcy.

Maria led me inside her house, in which she lived alone. And although she lived alone, not a single room felt empty or starved of attention. The entrance, had a staircase in the middle that split left and right, leading to a wraparound landing, with doors spotted all around it. A chandelier hung from the ceiling, and sweet wooden frames that still smelt of freshly cut sandalwood and palm leaves, held pictures and paintings to the magnolia walls. The living room was at the back of the house and connected to the kitchen, which revolved around a large marble island. The entire back wall was glass, bathing the room in a golden glow as the sun was now setting. "I'm sorry I didn't ask before coming, I just... This is kind of... you know... a big deal." She took my hand and we sat upon the olive-green sofa side by side. "Don't you apologise." She placed her hand on the side of my face as if trying to familiarise the way I looked, through touch. "How long is your Dad gone for?" She asked, her face now at peace. "Two weeks. He left Yesterday." She nodded. "Then stay with me for one. Will you stay with me for one of them?" She asked, holding her breath a little. "I would love to. I've missed you." I trembled, tears now stinging my eyes. "I never knew it was possible to miss somebody you don't even remember meeting." I looked away from her and out of the window, spotting a brown and white horse. "He's beautiful... Is he supposed to be in your garden?" I giggled, seeing her place her head in her hands and laugh to herself sort of hysterically. "No. No. He. Is. Not. That's Bubbles. He's really very sweet but he is shy of the other horses and jumps the stable fences almost every day." She quit her distraction and faced back to me. "I'm still a little confused... Will you tell me what happened from the start, sweet one?" I nodded and told her everything. She sat silently and listened to it all, her mouth very slightly open.

 When I had finished, the moon was out and the room was shadowed with a refreshing, cleansing breeze. She sat forward. "I made a casserole." She grinned, gesturing to her apron and then the slow cooker on the island. It was only then that I realised the rush of homely, cooked scents were so very present. I was expecting her to say pretty much anything else. "It smells wonderful... Are you okay?" She nodded and touched her lips with the tips of her fingers, and then stood up. "You must be famished. Let's get some food in you." She bustled over to the kitchen, and started cluttering around busily, pouring ladles of hearty goodness into white, china bowls. "Why don't we eat, and then talk. Let's pause all the dramas outside and eat. Just for a little while. Then I will tell you everything. Okay?" I nodded uncertainly and followed her to the dining room.

How could I possibly sit there, spoon in hand, and pretend nothing had happened? As I ate more, not asking became easier. The chunks of chicken were cooked to perfection, flaking wonderfully and the veggies that floated around with them softly crunched and spilled flavours I had never experienced in my whole life. When we had finished our meals, Maria stood up, moving out of the way of a picture of her and another woman, who was perhaps two inches shorter. They both wore matching outfits. Dresses of mustard colour, with sunflower patterns on the skirt. I disregarded my original question ("Could you please tell me more about the diary?") And instead, snatched the frame. The wood from which it was made felt rough and I assumed it had been hand made. At the bottom of it was painted grass and little, tiny flowers. "This is her! This is my mum! I drew pictures of

By Felicity Jayne

her in this skirt! I thought I had made it up because I was so little! Oh my goodness, Maria, can I see her? Please take me to her, I can't believe it!" I exclaimed, dancing around the room with the picture, looking at the face of the woman I had waited so desperately to hold. Maybe she would ring the doorbell any second, come through the door holding a loaf of home made bread and drop it as soon as she saw me.

Maria carefully held out her hand to me from across the room. "Take my hand." She spoke with a note of sadness in her usually melodic tone. Her eyes looked teary. I walked across to her and took her hand. "That lady in the picture *is* your Mum. I loved her... deeper than I have loved anybody in my whole life. She was like a sister to me." I dropped her hand. "Was? What happened? Did you fall out?" I asked, still smiling, but slighter. "On the day she wrote that diary entry, she... She tried to chase after your Father's car to get you back. He... Lost control." She was crying now. "And she... She died, sweetheart. Your Mama died. Your Father made me promise not to tell a soul or he would..." She gazed into the distance, and I swayed, looking around me for the best place to throw up. Buzzing lights crowded my vision, radiating darkness until all I saw was an empty void of nothingness. I fell to the floor and awoke some time later, with Maria beside me.

"Hey. Hey, can you hear me?" I looked around, remembering where I was, and all that had happened with an awful tugging feeling in my stomach. "I can hear you." I said blankly, lying their motionlessly. My eyes felt heavy, and I longed to just fall asleep right there on the hard floor. "I'm here. I'm right here." Maria insisted, rubbing my arms the way you do to warm yourself up. "I shouldn't feel this sad." I sighed. "I can't be heartbroken over something I never expected to have." She looked at me with huge melancholy eyes.

"Of course you can. She was... Wonderful. You look just like her. You do." She smiled, wiping tears from my face with her hand. "And while you're here, I can tell you everything about her. I wrote a book of our stories that I hoped I could read you someday. I know we haven't seen each other in a very long time. You won't even remember me. I knew you for such a short time, but I have missed you always. Every day I heard from you was a good day. You're so kind and smart and funny. Mary would be so proud." She helped me sit up, and I wrapped my arms around her. Around the one piece of my mum I had left. Every part of me ached and every part of relief stripped from my soul was replaced with fear. "I don't ever want to go home." I choked, holding onto Maria tightly. "Run away and take me with you. Somewhere safe. Where you can make your casseroles and teach me how to make them too. Somewhere where I can write and talk and be with you. Maria, I'm so scared." She held me back. "Oh." She gave a great sigh and began to cry too. "Sweetheart, we can't run. I can't run. It's safe for the both of us, if, and only if, you fly home in a week, and never talk of this again. Do you promise? Will you do that for me?" I nodded and buried my face into her raspberry smelling blonde hair, crying bitterly until I had no tears left. When, and only when, Maria had managed to bring out a slight smile in me, did she lead me upstairs into a bedroom with pretty pastel teal walls and a window seat overlooking the back garden. She switched on a white lamp and threw the covers back so I could slip within them, and then tucked me in. "My bedroom is directly next to this one. If you need anything at all then you just call me, and I'll come right back. You shine so brightly." She sat on the edge of the bed and sighed dreamily. "You know, sometimes a door closes. And the whole world just opens right up."

That's a piece of wisdom I never, ever forgot. It's so incredibly true. Sometimes, you'll go looking for one thing and find so much more. Your life will rarely evolve into exactly what you want it to become. But that doesn't mean it isn't a life worth living.

Still feeling like my insides were a cocktail of messy fear and sadness, I laid back onto the pillows. "Thank you for everything. I love you a lot." I took her hand, and she took mine back, and squeezed gently, three times. "I love you more." As she left, she gently closed the door, leaving it open a few inches, so the light from the landing could still provide a little, much needed comfort.

Dreamland was a frequently visited destination that sleepless, restless night. I awoke repeatedly, given just seconds to gasp for reality before I was submerged back into my nightmares. There was this one dream that was worse than all the others, though looking back on it now, all I see and hear are blurred shapes, and loud noises. A slash of Rosie's pink coat. A whack of my father's hand on her face. His screams. Oh, how he screamed. And Rosie's bleeding cries that came with those screams, heard by nobody accept the aloof fir trees that cloaked our house.

I awoke.

"We have 12 days. Now, I personally would much rather spend them making fun memories together, but if you want to sleep in for two weeks that's also fine!" Maria called mockingly from the door. "I'm thinking we get Bubbles out of the yard, bake until our hearts are content, then I'll take you for a sunset walk in the meadow. What are you thinking?" She smiled, clearly bothered by this whole series of events, but intent on making the best of them. She did that a lot. She even had a tea towel in the kitchen that said, 'when life gives you lemons, make lemonade.' "I'm thinking that sounds wonderful." I smiled back. She left so I could change, and after doing so, I reached for my phone, suddenly aware I hadn't updated Darcy since boarding the second plane, and with a pang, noticed that she had read the single message from the previous day and not replied. I messaged her again, asking if she was alright, but this one didn't even go through to her phone. Feeling sick with worry, I tied my hair up before washing my face with cold water and lavender face wash. The bathroom was painted a mauve colour and everything from the hand towels to the soap dish fit the desired aesthetic. Even more generic quotes could be found upon the cute signs, painted with pastel colours and great care, that hung on the walls.

I then headed downstairs to find Maria in the garden. She looked so perfect, hugging Bubbles' fluffy neck, that she looked as if she perhaps wasn't even real. I put my boots on and wandered towards her, starstruck, while my white floral print dress swayed tiredly in the hot breeze. "Who is it, Bubbles?" Maria asked in the creatures ear. She spoke to him like a child in need of kindness. For a moment, I became jealous of the horse. He had known nothing but Maria and her kindness his whole life. He spent his existence, feeding off of juicy, healthy grass and sunbathing as he pleased. That jealous feeling soon changed to intense love however, the second I placed my hand on his head. His fur was shiny and unlike any other horse I had known. Not course and prickly one bit. He nuzzled me caringly, and Maria giggled. "He knows you're sad. He's trying to make you feel good." She sniffed, hugging me awkwardly, as if it were forbidden, and only okay to do so when I was in such a state, like the previous evening. "Good morning, gorgeous one. This dress is stunning on you. You look fit for a ball. A real princess." She stroked the shoulder of the dress. "Thank you. But you really win the prize for stunning." I smiled, admiring her beige and white striped dress. She rocked a trendy, graceful look, with ease. We led Bubbles back to his stable and fed the other three horses together. Fresh hay and flowers in the hanging baskets made the air smell divine. Maria taught me gently, how to feed the animals, and then we spoke for a while in the darling stables, sat on crates and overturned buckets, in the empty pen, furthest away from the front door. The place was lit by hypnotic hanging lights that resembled lanterns and hung from the

ceiling in a line down the middle, above where
you could walk through, and see horses sleeping
either side. There were two doors either end, one
for entering and one exiting into a grazing field
that contained a shelter stacked high with hay.

"I first met your Mum when I was nineteen. My
mum is a nurse, and so was your Grandmother.
We met at one of their work functions, and never
looked back." She began, twiddling a piece of
straw in her fingers. "It was a ridiculously boring
party, so we decided to sneak out and hit the
town. We went into this one bar, called 'The
O'Toole's'. It was this little Irish place, that sold
the most incredible drinks. We got so drunk that
these two guys drove us home. We had never
met them before. And one of them, was your
Father. He was friends with us for a while. In fact,
he dated Maria before he dated me. I know how
dysfunctional that sounds but... There's nothing
functional about him. I'm sure you're aware of
that."
"You mean Mary? Not Maria. *You're* Maria,
silly." I shivered, oppressed now with the
memory of finding out that my father was the
reason I had no Mother, and slightly worried my

sudden appearance had broken the closest thing I had left to one. He had orphaned his own baby. "Can we pretend he doesn't exist?" I asked, quickly. Maria turned to face me. "He wasn't always this way. He was once a very kind man. But his mind got to him and... Alcohol can change a person. But we don't have to talk about that. Is there anything you want to know? About her? About me?" Her eyes had me held in a brace so strong it was invisible to any other human eye. I was flooded with affection for her constantly. She was, in an instant, my home. I felt rebirthed the second she set eyes upon me. I had never been looked at with such pure, pristine, powerful love. "Did she like strawberries?" I asked. "Did she like strawberries?" Maria repeated to herself, her voice like that of a birds morning call. "She never let a day go past without eating them. Why?" My heart felt warm.
"I can't ever get enough of them. Peanut butter?"
"Oh she hated that stuff. The smell of it made her quite sick."
"Are you kidding? Me too! I can't even look at it. This is fun... Okay... Lemon cake?" We continued that game all the way home.

The Field Where All The Flowers Grow

When we got there, we baked muffins and breads and pies and cooked steamed vegetables, brown rice, and salmon for dinner, all the while talking about everything under the sun. I could've lived in that day forever. Those letters that brung me such elation had been transformed into something larger than life. A hero. An unstoppable maternal force that showed nothing but strength in the most gentlest ways. If you closed your eyes right now, and I asked you to picture the one person that meant the most to you. The one person who you knew would be your muse forever. Your inspiration. Your idol. Then you too, would see your Maria.

After dinner, and washing the dishes, while singing little tunes together, we walked to the field where all the flowers grew. Up close it was even more regal. Long, cool grass tickled our legs playfully as we wandered through the perfected, rainbow mess. Each and every flower I laid eyes on sparked with individual personality. The poppy leaves fluttered delicately like butterfly wings against a current while the lavender stood firm, in bundles, showing off their dreamy scent. The sunset was one large whisp of blue, pink, and yellow, melting into one another like a triple ice cream on a hot summers day. When we reached an empty, softer piece of ground, Maria laid down and I laid sleepily beside her, reaching for, and clasping her hand. She took mine back and held it protectively, despite the most dangerous thing near us being a single bumble bee. "I love you." I sighed wistfully, knowing I'd have to say those three words as many times as humanly possible before I could never speak them to her again. "Oh, I love you so very much too." She smiled pensively, looking up at the sky and giving my hand a little squeeze three times. "Your Mum used to do that to you when you were little. Three squeezes for I love you. She loved you more than anything in this world. I hope you know that." I faced her.

"I do. I feel it inside of my heart with every beat." As the sun went down, we made our way back towards the house, leaving the rich soil, mischievous weeds, and luscious flowers behind us, knowing with a true comfort, they would be there Tomorrow.

As we walked onwards, clinging to one another, despite it slowing us down, two small lights wiggled in the distance. Maria halted. "Nobody drives past here at this time. It's a dead end." Her voice was bone dry and scared, and with her words, came my realisation that the lights were headlights, and the car that held them had stopped right outside the house. "It's not him. It's not him. It's not him." I trembled, my legs shaking and weak, feeling as if gravity had just intensified and was trying to drag me down, beneath the earth.

Out of the car exited three people. Two women and a man. They were, at this second, too far away for me to distinguish. The man, turned sinisterly to us and pointed, bellowing with a deep, familiar, gruff, whiskey tainted voice. "COME ON BABY! COME TO ME NOW!" I stood, stunned.
"That isn't anybody, Jordan!" Rosie squealed, with a recognisable, shrill, mortified tone.
"They're just trees!" My heart dropped into my stomach.
"You disgust me woman!" My father spat at her, hitting her repeatedly until she fell to the floor. It's horrible to see anybody get hurt, but this particular act of violence stuck with me forever.

By Felicity Jayne

The way he hit her; was like she was cold blooded. Plummeting his fist into her body and back out again, as if he were kneading some dough to death. With every blow came a gruelling, startling, piercing scream. The scream of a woman that had been beaten down for years, and ground to almost nothing, so she could be used as a pawn in a wicked man's game. "You lie to me again!" He screeched, "And I'll kill you! I swear, I'll kill you!" While they were too focused on themselves, Maria pulled me to the side, jumped the fence and then lifted me over with her, before running as fast as she could with her hand in mine, toward the gate that led from the field to the dirt road. Then she squeezed my hand. Three times. "I. Love. You."

Chapter four –

At school, whenever our class got too noisy, our teachers would yell. No matter how severe or minor the yell was, I'd flinch and be out of focus for the rest of the lesson. I bet they wondered but they never did ask. My father would have sporadic outbursts over the drop of a faucet my whole life. It was impossible to tell when he was going to snap. Living in that house was like trying to walk through an autumn forest floor without making a single sound. Sometimes an entire tree could collapse, and the monster would stay asleep. But some days, the rustle of a single leaf could provoke it to terrorise everything in its grasp for no good reason. I had heard him scream an unfathomable amount of times before. But not like this. Never like this. When he discovered we had made a run for it, he let out this treacherous, globe shaking, heart wrenching, nauseating roar. "IF THE TWO OF YOU DON'T GET BACK HERE IN THE NEXT FIVE SECONDS, I'LL SHOOT!" I stopped dead in my tracks like somebody had pressed pause on the scene. My ears rung. Maria dragged me onwards with an unbreakable strength as I gasped for air, and freedom, and life. "Shhhh," She hushed, hurrying me along. "I've got you; nobody is getting shot today-"

Then the sound came.

Muffled but certain. Piercing but cancelled out by its own terror. Then again. Not one bit less scarier than the first. Then silence. "We're okay, we're okay!" Maria sung, as we reached the gate. She gathered me beside her and pressed me up against the bricks either side of the spiked black bars, so any harm aimed at me would hurt her first. I fought against her, wanting to take any shot, blade or word thrown her way. But she calmly resisted, trying to enter her code onto the keypad. "It isn't working!" She stammered, trying over and over again. A cold sweat rinsed me, and I looked behind me at the dark, twisted alleyway formed by sinister, mangled tree trunks and branches. Each twig had its own role in the choreographed dance of nature - some twisting, some reaching aimlessly into the night until a hellish tunnel was formed. The trees enclosed darkness and nothing else, though as I stared, petrified into the void of eerie unknown I swore I

could see shapes form from within the
nothingness.

"I don't understand!" Maria hissed with gritted
teeth. She looked like a deer in the headlights,
her fly away wisps of hair reflecting how wildly
frustrated she was. Then something went off
inside her and she realised what she had to do.
"You can get over." She gripped my shoulders
and kissed my face longingly, her eyes forcing
shut as if she couldn't bear what was about to
happen. "I can lift you up. You go over. You run
now. It's time to run, baby. Run as fast and as far
as you can. For both of us-"
"NO!" I sobbed, clawing at her cardigan, and
refusing to let go. "I'd rather die than be without
you. I'll never get over this. If you make me go,
I'll never smile again." She clasped me close to
her heart and I could hear it beat frantically. I
looked back into the darkness behind us and
became suddenly aware of the silence
surrounding the place in which we were prepared
to take our final breath. "It's too quiet." I
whispered, quivering like an innocent bunny
under fire. "Who got shot?" Maria shook her
head, touching her forehead briefly. "I don't

know." I asked the question, but I wasn't truly listening. I had clenched my hands together and dropped to the moss carpet beneath me. "What are you doing?" She sniffed. Her voice broke off in huge chunks as her tears streamed down her angelic face. "I'm praying that no matter what. We stay together. I wouldn't be the person I am Today if you hadn't shown me so much of who I want to be-"

"YOU STAY AWAY!" Maria yelped, her voice burning through the cold fragments of moonlight that shadowed us. It was then I realised she hadn't asked me what I was doing. She had asked Rosie. She stood, perhaps twenty meters away from us. Dressed in red. No. White. She was dressed in a white suit, saturated with blood. "I won't hurt you! I didn't know anything until he told me we were on a private plane to Texas and not Hawaii." Her voice broke off horribly and she was beaten to an almost unrecognisable form. "I know what he changed the code to. 4242. Try it!" She spoke in a hybrid of whisper and skittish scream.

Maria blindly felt for the numbers and entered them sceptically, refusing to break eye contact with my stepmother. The gate beeped and then swung open, and we both gave tremendous sighs of relief. "Journey-" Rosie had dropped to the floor. She was week and shot. Blood gushed from the hole in her shoulder and ran into her silk clothing, highlighting streaks of crimson across it. "I'm glad you found your Mama. And I'm sorry I wasn't a better one to you." She breathed in once, sporadically, and then flopped motionless to the ground. It was the first encounter we had ever had where she barely spoke. She hadn't even been told what Jordan had done to my sweet Mother, Mary. "Jordan Hunt is a smart man. A very smart man. She could be playing dead or sent to fool us." Maria gasped, heaving the gate open. "But if what she says is true, there's not a chance in hell I'm going to let this lady die here alone."

I took over holding the gate, while Maria lifted Rosie's small body into her arms, and carried her out onto the dirt road. Another set of headlights sliced through the night, lurching towards us with intense speed. I flinched and helped Maria hold Rosie. We just stood there, in disbelief, as a miracle happened before our bloodshot, weary eyes.

The car was a pristine, pearly-white truck with black polished seats. Or as I viewed it in that moment, and for every moment after, until I closed my eyes for one final time, a chariot from heaven. "MUM?" Maria sobbed, as it slowed beside us. "Jordan came, he shot his wife in my front yard and is trying to kill us." The lady opened the door urgently, pulling Rosie inside. "GET IN THE BACK, QUICKLY NOW!" Unaware of what was happening at all, I was thrust gently into the far passengers seat, and the second Maria closed the door, we were off. "I got a security alert and came right over, sweetheart. Thank goodness for technology." Maria's Mother said, colouring in the gap in our knowledge nicely. She was entirely every bit as beautiful as Maria. Her eyes were a startling ocean colour and her hair, sandy and grey all at once. Her face bore lines of bravery, wisdom and strength and her hands drove us away from disaster with calm, controlled ease. "Is this her?" She breathed so quietly, as if the sound only threatened to travel from her blush lips to our ringing ears. Maria looked at me apologetically then spoke the next few words very carefully. "It is." I frowned and blearily interrupted their exchange. "What's happening?" I saw Maria's Mother's eyes graze me from the mirror above her. "We're going to drive to my house. It's very safe there, your Dad doesn't know where I live. I'm a nurse. I'm going to help this lady next to me and call the police. Are you hurt, young one?" She asked with tender care. "We're okay?" I asked looking up at Maria, bewildered at how easily we seemed to have escaped death. "We're okay. We're okay." She looked up at her Mother. "We're just shaken. Not hurt." She turned to me. "Sweetheart, this is my mother. Her name is Julie." Darkness.

When I next awoke, I was on a cushy sofa in a familiar room that echoed with panic. I wasn't sure where it was familiar from. It gave me the same feeling as the one you get when you read the first line of your favourite book for the first time in forever. Or hugging somebody you have been kept from for so long. My vision was distorted for a moment, and I could feel an unpleasant pressure building behind my eyes. Screams of muffled pain bounced off the walls and I gave a shaky exhale, remembering where I was, and why I was there. "She's awake! She's awake-" Maria startled. "You'll be the death of me, goodness!" She cried, bringing a blanket she had laid over me, further up so I was almost entirely covered. "Rosie?" I asked, breathlessly. "She's being stitched up. My mum is the best at what she does, she'll be okay. She lost a ton of blood though, so we called an ambulance. Trouble is, we live so far out of the way, it'll take them much longer to get here than you'd expect. You were in and out for an awfully long time. Do you remember anything?" I shook my head. "Are we safe? You're sure that we're safe?" She nodded definitely.

"Yes. Yes, we are very safe." Julie entered suddenly.

"The police are coming too." She informed us with a shiver.

"Maria? Are you going to tell them about how he killed my mum?" I asked innocently, reaching for her trembling hand. Julie tilted her head and missed the sharp warning look Maria had given to her. As if following a stage lighting cue, the room darkened, further. "Your Mama is fine, sweetheart. She must be concuss, did she hit her head?" Julie came closer, sitting on the edge of the sofa and feeling around my hair for any clue of trauma. "She thinks you're Maria." She smiled, sadly. My stomach churned horribly. "Maria died a long time ago. Your Dad killed her in a driving accident about 14 years ago. She was trying to save you from your Father and bring you back to your Mum. Mary. Mary Elizabeth Pinnock."

 She turned to my mother.

"Mary. Tell her who you are. Gently. Gentle reminders may bring her back to us a little." But she didn't speak. She didn't move.

There *was* a Maria. She *was* my mother's best friend. But my mother wasn't the one who had died that night, with her blood painting the pavement with a forever tainted memory of pain and decay and lost hope, as it mixed in with the dust, the dirt, and the gravel. Maria was.

 I grew up in know of my mother's name, so in my dad's grovelling threat he forced her to contact me only through Maria's. Every letter a scared lie. Every word and story a glittering façade. True but cryptic.

I sat up, dazed, but if we're being entirely honest, the thought had crossed my mind before, as I'm sure it did yours, before this point. I suppose I just put it down to my wild, often untamed imagination. "I'm. So sorry. I was only trying to protect us both. If I had told you... I was so scared. I... I wanted to tell you – I was going to tell you – before you left. I just didn't know how. I understand if you're upset. It was a cowardly move and I-" I pressed my finger over her lip softly and wrapped my arms around her neck. Julie stepped back, confused. Not for long however, as she was soon distracted as easily as a kitten to a laser pen.

Through the cracks in the shutters, a golden glowing light seeped. It flashed around the room. "They don't have their sirens on-" I began, wearily as Julie ran to greet the police. Her footsteps faded, and then loudened with a hushed intent. "I'm sorry." A voice came from behind me. I turned to find Rosie with her phone in her hand. We all looked at her with a feeling of intense betrayal. "I helped you..." Maria thought out loud, wistfully and fading away. "He'd kill me. He always finds a way. You know that. He said if... If I told him where to find you... He'd let me run. I won't have to see him ever again." She sounded sadistically at peace. Like the mistake she had made was as simple as buying the wrong brand of washing up liquid. There was an off-putting calm about how she began to circle us. I stood frozen with my mama and Grandmother now.

"Let us go. Let us leave. Please Rosie-" I said, trying to match her unexplainable attitude. It was rapidly evolving. A tear, then a smile, then a laugh, then a sniff and a deep breath. "I'm afraid I can't let you do that, honey." Her voice was silky like poison but jagged with exhaustion and premature regret. She was so broken, and that broke my heart more than anything. Thunderous bangs sounded and the front door fell . The golden glow was extinguished, and all the lights stayed out. A ragged, limping silhouette of my father slugged towards us in the little moonlight that shone through the frame in which the door had once stood.

"She stays with me." Maria cried out, her voice strangled by the hands of inevitable death and every fear we are trained to accompany it with. As if the clouds above had accidently dropped an eternity of water on Texas in that moment, rain began hammering the windows. "My daughter stays with me." Maria bit. "I won't tell a soul anything you've ever done. Not to Me. Not to Maria. Not to anyone. But she stays with me. You leave now. You walk out that door and I never hear your voice or see your face again."

A morbidly eerie pause laid on the room, suffocating us under its startling tension.

"You won't have to hear my voice or see my face ever again. That part is true." He snarled, pained but present. "Mary. Darling." He laughed a little to himself now. His teeth were so ironically, pure white, I could almost see them through the thick, murky darkness. "This isn't a life. Wasting away alone, on a ranch. Writing letters to a kid you birthed 17 years ago that didn't even know you were alive until a few days ago." He turned towards me. I couldn't see him well, but his breath infected my breathing air and moistened my blushed cheek. "And you. I tried. And tried. But no matter how hard I tried; I could never get rid of the memory of what I had done without getting rid of you. And I still think that bitch- that you all, deserve what you got. But the damn woman haunts my every move. So ladies, if you please-" His speech was slurring, and I gave an audible wince as he set a blood-soaked hand on my cheek. "Let us get this all over with. You won't feel a thing. Oh and... Tell Darcy hi for me." He growled in my ear, thrusting me to the floor alongside my mother. I looked around frantically, but saw no sight of Julie, and realised as my eyes caught Rosie's, he hadn't even addressed her since he had entered the room. I let My mum hold onto me as her hands fumbled across my body as if she were preparing to hold me forever. And then it had sunk in.

Tell Darcy hi. Tell Darcy hi *for me.*

A shot fired from the gun in his outstretched hand. Nobody yelled. Nobody cried. There was utter silence in the room, accept from the suicidal raindrops plummeting from the heavens for what felt like an hour but was only a few short seconds. And then my stepmother's body fell onto mine, and I knew in my heart, that she was truly remorseful. She had literally taken a bullet for me. One shot and she had completed the purest act of the human heart.

Another shot. And it was all for nothing.

Chapter five –

I fell loosely back, slumped against the wall behind me. Blue lights encased us, and for a second I considered closing my eyes and letting go. I felt like I could have. But I knew I shouldn't. It didn't matter where I was going to go, it wouldn't be heaven without my mum. Within seconds, three police officers had burst through the hall, and launched themselves at my father as he shot aimlessly in the dark, luckily only killing a placemat and a few chairs. "My daughter is shot!" Mary sobbed. Julie suddenly slammed on the lights from where she had been hiding and raced over. Two of the policemen cuffed my father and scraped him from the floor with ease, despite his reckless resistance and earth-quaking bellows. Julie set her hand firmly over the blood fountain which was sprouting from my hip. "You're okay, angel." She hushed, as My mama wiped the tears from my eyes. I was unsure of how I was supposed to process what had just happened. I reached my hand gingerly to the side of me and rested it on Rosie's sprawled out blonde hair. The ambulance pulled up and two medics rushed inside. "She stays with me. She stays with me." Mama muttered over and over again, burying her face in my shoulder. "Try and bring her back." I croaked, to the first aiders assisting me. They both gave a disregarding look to Rosie. "Sweetie, she doesn't have a pulse." One spoke softly. The policewoman that remained with us, gently removed my hand from her hair. "I don't want them to take her away." I sighed; my eyes bleeding with the tears of a broken heart that hurt far worse than the bullet plunged in my hip. "There's no exit wound, we need to get her to the hospital right away, Mam. Are you her Mother?"

"Yes. Yes I am. Will you take us there now?"

"Right away." I was strapped to a gurney and placed in an ambulance that drove at the speed of light to the nearest hospital, possibly twenty minutes away. The stiff and ridged platform beneath me dug into my spine and my leg was now wet with wrongly spilled blood.

When we arrived, there was an incredible commotion, and one of the many machines I had been hooked up to, started making a different noise, scaring everyone around me into action. A mask was placed over my face. "Think of some place nice, honey, everything is going to be just fine."

Think of some place nice.

The pond weed danced in the same winds that wafted dandelion seeds to the floor like warm, fluffy snowflakes. Colour rinsed the picture like the rain that had fallen the night before, and some of the roses still had drops smothering their petals. I could see my face in each mirroring spec of water. I looked healthy, and realised all the pain I had been enduring was gone. A soft, warm hand slipped into mine. I didn't have to turn and see who was beside me.

I knew Darcy's grip like no other.

"You knew I'd find the diary." I said, observantly. "I know he made you. It's okay. I forgive you." Then the hand was gone, and the shadow beside me combusted into a huge pearl of white light, that birthed the purest and most alluring warmth all around it. Then, just as I thought it couldn't look anymore stunning, it burst into a trillion golden pieces that flew around in little fluorescent disks, casting a spell of glitzy golden film over the picture. I laid down on the soft bed of grass and felt the luscious, mossy carpet tickle my fingers. The flowers were somehow even more precious here, and there were new kinds too, that I don't feel I can even speak of, for their beauty is irreplaceable, and not to be described in any matter, for fear of not justifying their impeccable beauty, in our world. I felt the presence of everybody I had ever loved. I longed to stay there forever, but just as I closed my eyes, a beeping sound occurred, rattling through my bones and my hip began to hurt again. There was no pain in that place. Only good. That's how I knew I was back.

The room was simple and bleak. A sad, little forest painting hung on the wall in front of me, attempting to brighten the atmosphere a little. It didn't. "You're okay. You're good. You're safe." Julie insisted as soon as my eyes opened. She had her hand on my forearm. "Where's Mar-" I remembered. "Where's Mama?"
"She's talking to the police. She's been with them for an awfully long time. She should be back

soon."

"Where is... he?" I stammered.

"In the far wing, surrounded by lots of security guards, my love." She stroked my hair. "This is not how I dreamed of meeting my granddaughter after 14 years of being kept from her." She sighed. "How do you feel now?" I thought for a second.

"I saw Darcy. When I was asleep. I was in the field... the one where all the flowers grow, at home. I didn't see her actual face, but she held my hand and then burst into this ball of warm light. I think... It was real." A little startled, she looked towards the door. My mother walked through it, as if scripted, and then hurried to my side as soon as she glimpsed I was awake.

"Thank God for you, thank God for you!" She sung tearily. "I saw Darcy. When I was asleep. I was with her, in the flower field. She held my hand and then turned into a huge shiny beam of light." She stopped dead in her tracks. "That's... Magical." She said uncertainly, looking at her own Mum. "Did the police tell you what happened to her?" I asked, feverishly. "They don't know yet. I informed them about his hints to what he had done. Told them everything.

The Field Where All The Flowers Grow

About us, Maria, last night. I'm so happy you're okay. I'm so sorry that this happened. I'll never let you out of my sight again."

I was questioned by the police, in my hospital room, alone, that evening. Recalling every detail, made my heart throb and sting. I missed Darcy and knew I would be forever haunted, by Rosie's dying image. I had a bruise on my cheekbone where her corpse had smashed to the floor and sprawled over me. Still warm. Blood still pumping. Yes, the bruise would fade, but the memory never would. I thought my life, from that moment forward, would be an unescapable nightmare, that I'd never be able to fully wake from. If I had died, I could have stayed with Darcy in bliss, and waited for my mama to follow, when her time came. But instead, I was forced under spotlights, followed by cameras, and plastered against my will, on the front of every local newspaper.

That night, after the police had asked their questions, I was left alone. My mum and Grandmother had gone to grab us dinner, though I didn't have much appetite. My mind kept spinning like a washing machine, accept there was no laundry to be found – only bad thoughts and memories and ideas. Nobody knew what had happened to Darcy, so my mind had pounced at the opportunity to guess. With every blink I saw a different crime scene. Had she been spiked and left to die alone in a back alley of a bar, clutching her stomach and foaming at the mouth, preventing her from calling for help? Did the shadows of the night swarm her like beasts and shield her from the eye of any pedestrian until it was too late, and she was discovered the next day, her clothes wet and gritty with dirt from the rainfall? Or did my father send someone to drown her, in the river behind our house? Would she be discovered by our sweet neighbour, Percy, as he walked his puppy at the crack of dawn? Mangled and strangled by underwater weeds, her skin embedded with filth and grime. These were all ridiculously silly thoughts. My father was a smart man. Darcy would never be found. And I shouldn't have worried because I knew she was okay. I had seen her. As my eyes began to close, the sound of high heels could be heard, clip-clopping down the hard floored corridor. The beat of the footsteps grew closer, and with its closing proximity, grew an unsettling familiarity. As if each step was a knock at an unstable, wooden door. An unstable, wooden door, about to give in.

Another shot. As if the first batch had left us famished for more.

Scarlet blood sprayed with unjustified ease, upon the little window on the closed door. The thud of the security guard outside hitting the floor, as his head spewed and leaked with all sorts of liquids, horrified me beyond belief. I closed my eyes and laid very still, wishing, and praying and hoping that this was a nightmare from which I would soon awake. The door creaked open, the sound like a dying groan. Pained and helpless. More footsteps occurred now and through the darkness of my eyes being closed, I could still make out a shadow. As I breathed, the itching scent of fake floral perfume tickled my nose. "Goodnight." Helen's voice poured from her mouth into my ears like steam. Smooth and withering all at once. I opened my eyes and found her plunging a needle into the drip attached to me, via a huge needle. Five hundred ml of sodium pentobarbital. Without a second thought I ripped the canular from my hand and reached clumsily, for the 'help' button on my bedside, though these actions were far too late, for Helen had seen me immediately. To my greatest relief, I had jammed the button and an alarm had sounded. "Lie down. It's okay. It's okay." Helen ordered with a peculiar calmness. I had sat up, but she was forcing me back down with her arm. It didn't take much force; I was sleepy and bleary eyed. "It won't hurt if you just let me do it now. Just close your eyes. Go see Darcy now-" A crashing sound broke her feigned, chill mood. We both flinched and without a second thought, she gathered me in her arms. I tried to scream but I was so terrified, no sound came out. My hip cramped and stung, as she held onto me tightly. It felt as if somebody had stuck a lit match within the wound. I was astonished at her unhuman strength, especially considering how much shorter than me she was.

A small crowd of nurses and police officers screeched to a stop, forming a mini pile up, at the door. Every single one of their faces, pale and aghast. Drenched in sweat and gasping for air, I tried to bat Helen away, but my limbs were feeble, and she had pointed a gun to my head.

The Field Where All The Flowers Grow

The metal was cool against my hot skin and for a second, before I processed what it was, I was grateful for the relief of the irritated, blotchy, panicked rash, it had brought. "Move back, or I'll shoot!" She bellowed, stunning them into silence. She sprung forward a step. Then another. Each move she made was calculated and fierce but motivated only by fear. I wasn't sure which game my father was playing with her, but I felt pitiful knowing it would only end in death for everyone but him. As we reached the threshold of the door, Helen gave a few aimless shots into the crowd and proceeded dragging me from the building, with her hand plastering my mouth shut, until we were close enough to the car for her to throw me in the back and slam the door. Carelessly, she threw herself into the drivers seat and immediately sped into the night, desperate to escape the unescapable. I kicked and screamed, begging her to release me, but she cocked the gun and aimed it directly at my face. If she shot, I would certainly die. Though the fact she was only steering the car with one tired hand, didn't exactly fill me with confidence I was going to make it out of this alive, anyway.

By Felicity Jayne

I knelt on the back seats, holding my hip which had started to bleed again. Through the window behind me, I saw streaky lights that starred outwards into the darkness, groping for more space to lighten and love. Gold and blue and red. The hospital was growing smaller and smaller, but just as I gave up hope, and tears splashed my gown, I saw my mother emerge from the entrance and pelt into the drivers seat of a police car. Some officers hurried inside with her, and she hurtled towards us, sirens blearing and acting as an oddly comforting white noise.

Helen was muttering to herself and seemed to forget I was even in the car. Dust lined every surface I touched, and left a bitty, furry residue on my hands and knees. The window glass suffered scratches; some surfaced, others deep, as if rocks had been tossed and skimmed them cruelly. The rain hammered all around me, pleading to be let in. Each drop that flung itself at the glass, trickled into another, creating streams that looked like angry tears, wept from the eyes of a thousand innocent victims.

I was only able to see my mama driving, through the gaps between the window wiper clearing a space, and the drops filling it back up again with water marks, smears, and raindrop kisses. Instead of trying to make out her face, or the startling sirens that sliced through my pounding head, I focused on the shimmering glow of the headlights, tracing where they went with my finger, so I didn't feel so lost. We were on a busy, trafficked road now, cars swarming us like angry wasps, with a biting sting. The roads were slippery, so we skidded from side to side as if the car was an angry cradle. "Please let me go. Whatever he said, isn't true. He's gone now, the police have him. Just let me go. I'm scared. Please. I want my mum." I creased, crying, and shaking. My words to her were like bullets on titanium. There was no flinch, reaction, or sign that she had heard a single word of what I had said.

In an instant, my mother rapidly increased speed and dashed beside us. Slowly, and protected by the deafening sound of the wind rippling past us, I opened the window beside me, hoping Helen wouldn't notice. While driving, my amazing hero of a Mum swapped seats with the officer beside her and opened her *own* window. "MUM!

By Felicity Jayne

MUM! MAMA!" I screeched, until my throat bled. A metallic taste coated my mouth, and the thrusting, swerving motion of the car made me feel dizzy and faint. Helen was becoming more and more reckless with every passing second, and had her hand tightly around my ankle, the gun she was holding before, now in her lap. "HOLD MY HAND. REACH OUT, I GOT YOU!" My mother roared, desperately. I stretched out as far as I could, but our fingertips – wet with raindrops – only loosely brushed each other. She signalled to the driver to pull in closer and the vehicle neared a little. Still, I was trapped. "SHE WON'T LET GO OF ME!" I cried, blinding myself with tears and overwhelmed by the sheer volume around us. Horns were beeping left, right, and centre. "LOOK AT ME! WE'RE GETTING OUT OF THIS TOGETHER! OKAY? YOU DO WHATEVER YOU HAVE TO DO!" She ordered, her voice quivering and breathless. I turned to see Helen; her crazy eyes still glued on the road ahead. My heart thudded and thundered so forcefully I thought I might throw up. "Breathe." I told myself quietly, took one slow breath in, and then punched the hand holding my leg. I was released momentarily and used my other hand to hit my kidnapper in the face with my elbow. She gave a cry, and I used her brief distraction to grasp the gun from her lap. I aimed it at her. "I WON'T SHOOT, IF YOU LET ME GO!" I sobbed, solidifying my aim.

I knew I'd never be capable of taking a life, but hoped Helen wouldn't see through the threat, to the reality of the situation. "I'LL CRASH! I'LL KILL US BOTH!" Helen spat, as I turned, my arm still pointing the gun to her head as she tauntingly drove the car this way, then that way, so I almost fell from the window. "I'VE GOT YOU BABY!" My mum promised, reaching further. I leaned out of the window once more, and climbed, until my upper body was hanging over the vastly disappearing concrete beneath me. If I fell, I would be skinned by the roads and hit by another vehicle. I had to jump. I had to trust my mother. She had opened the entire door of her car now, so I had more space to jump into.

At last, I pushed forwards. She almost missed for a second, fumbling with the hospital gown, until she had a solid grip on my torso and was able to bring me to the safety of the other car. The door was slammed behind me as the car skidded into the resting lane of the motorway we had entered. Mama sat me on her lap, wrapping her arms around my stomach and applying pressure to my bleeding hip. I gave out a huge cry, unable to supress my agony. "Good job, sweetheart. You're my hero. We thought the security guard had you. I never would have- I'm so sorry-"

"We need to keep going and arrest that monster before we lose her." One of the officers insisted. "Shonda will wait with you. Back up is on the way. I can already see them behind us."

Shonda, the officer at the wheel, leapt from the car, and dragged me and my mother to the side of the road, safely. She was a fiery, gentle hearted and protective woman who I had the privilege of getting to know extremely well.

After a while, I began to look at that car chase as proof of the 'burnt toast theory,' or whatever it's called. The idea that while burning your toast may cause you frustration in the moment, had you not burnt the toast and ran a little late, you might have been hit by a car or mugged. Right place right time. I must admit however, I was not able to look on that situation with any light at all, while I was still clasped within it.

As I laid upon the cruel slip road, I could feel each and every sharp, jagged stone beneath me. Some pierced my skin and left cuts, while others scraped and bruised. The icy rain made the ground feel like unbearably cold ice on my bare back, for the gown was so thin and sodden, it functioned as a useless barrier. My lips were blue, and my skin white as snow. My mother leaned over me, with Shonda at the other side, acting as a shield from the rain. In that moment, it felt like we were the only three people in the entire universe. All I could see was darkness, and their faces. My mum's face was tearstained, and she wore the same dress I had seen her in yesterday morning, accept the hem was grass stained and creased with the stiffness that comes with the rain and filth you come across when your ex-husband chases you and your child into a muddy country lane at dusk, trying to kill you both.

The creamy lavender colour of the clip in Shonda's hair, reminded me of the flower field and my pain eased slightly. "Mama? I want to go back to the flower field with you." I said, dazed.

"Okay. Okay. Let's pretend we are there right now." She smiled, falsely. An ambulance and police car pulled up beside us. "What colour flowers do you see?" She asked, her voice coated in the desire to distract me. "Blue. Pink. Yellow. White. Red. Orange-"

"Good Job! What else do you see?"

"I can see the tall grass. And the trees. And the lake." My breathing slowed. "She's afraid." Shonda warned, as she joined my mother to the left of me, and let the medics assess the situation. "Here. Hold my hand." Shonda said, gifting her hand to mine. The medics were asking my mum questions, so she was unable to carry on the flower game. Shonda neared her face to mine and stroked the back of my hand with her thumb. "Tell me about this field, gorgeous." She smiled kindly, in a hushed whisper as if she understood the precious sacred, secrecy of the field already. "It's magical. You step inside it and all bad feelings go away. You can be anything you want to be, and you get a feeling of relief and comfort that is so deep, you don't feel as if anybody could ever be deserving of it."

"That sounds spectacular. I'd love to see it for myself." She gasped sweetly, her eyes widening with joy and her mouth grinning as if she were talking to a child much smaller. "You can come and see it. When this is all over." I promised, earnestly. A bunch of medical jargon that I failed to understand came from the mouths of the medics, then I was again, put into the back of an ambulance. Another mask placed over my face. And I was asleep, once more.

Chapter six –

The hospital room I was in when I awoke, was vastly different to the one I had previously encountered. The walls were painted a pretty, pale aqua, like a milder version of the colour of a turquoise rock. Not a hospital blue. A new, refreshing kind. This bed was far more comfortable. The sheets were cool and soft, unlike the frigid, cardboard-like material of the ones from the last bed. Though, what made the room the most beautiful, was my angel of a Mother. She stood, fluffing some flowers around in a vase, on the windowsill. The window was open and through it blew a delicate breeze that dreamily wafted her hair around with it. Each golden hair on her head teamed together, to look like a tamed mane of a majestic, Motherly lion - and she carried around with her that perfection that had me guessing weather she was truly real or not. She was too good to be true. She turned to me.

"I miss Darcy." I sighed wistfully, brutally aware of her absence again. I looked up at the ceiling, to find it was made of that pattern, as if a rake of sorts had been dragged through the plaster, while it were still wet and healing. My mama neared, taking quiet, pensive strides towards me. The cardigan she wore, was of a creamy, coffee colour and she smelt of Christmas. "I know. I miss her too. She was a delight. A little crazy, but... All the best people are, right?" She sat on the armchair right beside me and placed her hand on my forearm. "When can we go home?" I asked, letting my cheek sink into the pillow slightly as I looked over at her. "Soon, my love. Soon. Very soon." Shonda entered abruptly, spilling two cups of coffee on the floor, and disregarding them completely at the first glimpse of my open eyes. "There she is!" She jumped across the floor, dodging the coffee spills, and hugged my mum in an excited, congratulatory manner. "This is such a wonderful day!" I giggled lightly and closed my hand, imagining I was holding Darcy's.

She was the one who had taught me that dead doesn't necessarily mean gone, because people can live on through the memories you shared with them. So, as long as we keep the dead in our hearts, they will remain there, very much alive. In that moment I made a promise. A promise to Darcy that she would live through me, and that she would remain present in all my future accomplishments, scares, and sleepless nights. I would do this by ensuring I saw her in every fragile flap of a birds wings, the brightest star that is the first to appear each night, and in the mirror every time I looked in it and smiled. It was only after she left us that I realised just how alike we looked. I took immense comfort when my mum commented on our resemblance because I had always hoped I would grow to be as beautiful as Darcy.

The next few days of recovery and questioning were brutal but made bearable, by the simple, yet unforgettable acts of kindness from everyone around me. Julie, one day, when bringing me some changes of clothes, from my long forgotten suitcase in the living room at home, brought with her a hamper of the most vibrant fruit I had ever seen. Crunchy watermelon that burst with fruity, freshness as it exploded. Mangos with a silky smooth texture and sweet scent that lasted in the room forever, and refused to fade, stubbornly. Pears that blessed my tongue with the modest perfection of their taste. And of course, strawberries. Indescribable, sweet, rich

strawberries. "Save some for us, you two!"
Shonda cackled when she noticed my mother
and I had eaten most of them. "We can't help it,
they're so delicious!" My mother said, seriously,
before breaking into a laugh herself. Shonda was
a frequent guest at my bedside, and she never
came without a gift. A sneaky, little dessert, or a
flower to add to my vase. The best gift, however,
was her presence. The woman was hilarious and
brilliant. She told stories of such bravery and
strength with such a humble tone.

The nights were hideous, and accompanied by
nightmares, terrors and sometimes even sleep
walking. I hated having such a good imagination,
because yes, I could write stories, but I was also
burdened with the hardship of intrusive, and
unstoppable thoughts that always forced
themselves upon me with a bravery and
confidence I could never fight against. Darcy's
body. Rosie's blood. Jordan's screams. I revelled
in the fact the only thing I had in common with
my father was that our names began with the
same letter. I refused to associate myself with him
at all. The thought of him made me sicker than
the thought of peanut butter.

The night before the morning in which we drove home, my mother laid beside me, and we both stared restlessly at the ceiling. "We lost so much time." She said, with a looseness to her voice. I paused, took a deep breath, and then answered. "We can make it all up... Anyway, you were always with me. Just because you never held my hand, didn't mean you never... well... held my hand."

"How do you mean?"

"Well... You held my hand metaphorically. I would write to you when I was scared, or nervous, or sad, and you would always get me through whatever was wrong. You believed in me when I couldn't believe in myself. You showed up. You were here. And that's the most beautiful thing in the world." I reached for her hand and took it into my own. "You're a gift." I could hear the smile in her voice, and it delighted me so very much. She stayed by my side all night and awoke me excitedly the next morning.

We rolled the windows down and let the stream of rushing wind, billow through the car. Clouds bloomed and puffed out, swelling dramatically into the bright blueness of the sky. The moon hung protectively there all day, watching me for every second as if it were apologising for all of the terror it had let happen without intervening, in the nights previous. Taylor Swift was blasting so loudly from the speakers, that she blocked any negative thoughts from whispering in my ear and forcing themselves inside my brain. Together, me and my mother and Shonda sung along. All of us on a high. All of us unstoppable.

When we pulled up to the house, it looked even more exhilarating than before. It was as if the sanctuary had cleansed itself of every dark memory that had happened there. As if a constant, invisible tide hugged the homely walls, and washed away any negativity nearby. "Let me take you to the field, where all the flowers grow." I smiled back at Shonda who smiled and sighed dreamily. "I don't know if I want you walking all the way up there yet, brave one." My mother said, hesitantly, moistening her lips nervously. "But I have an idea." Her eyes lit up. "What? What's the idea?" I grinned, giggling as she mimed zipping her mouth shut, and throwing the key away. "Just wait! Wait and see! I'll show you in a little while!" She helped me walk slowly inside and sat me beside Shonda, on the couch that overlooked the yard. "This place is beautiful Mary!" She exclaimed, full of life as ever. "Thank you. I'm so happy to be here with the both of you. You're the absolute silver lining of our situation, Shonda." She smiled earnestly with her head tilted slightly and her hand on her heart.

Left by my sweet, newly found Grandmother, was a jug of fresh homemade, raspberry lemonade. My mother brought it, along with three precious crystal glasses, to the table. The ice clinked and chimed against the flutes, and we sipped as if we were dining at a fine restaurant somewhere very rich and fancy. The tiny bubbles emblazoned my mouth playfully with a fizzing, tingling bite. My mum opened the large screen doors and left through them, insisting she would be back in a few moments with her amazing idea.

Shonda sat beside me and took from her pocket a necklace with a silver chain and a sparkly, small, diamond pendant attached. She let the chain fall between her fingers loosely, as if it were the rarest, thinnest, most fragile snake in the entirety of existence. "That's lovely." I smiled, shyly. "Look inside." She handed it to me carefully and

helped me angle the pendant so the light behind
it allowed me to peer through the glass centre.
There was a picture of a man staring back at me
with the most humble grey eyes in the world.
Instinctively, I smiled at him and felt like he
could see me right back. The lines that traced his
face told stories of great courage and strength.
"Peter Barnbrook." Shonda sighed wistfully. "My
father. Clever, don't you think?" I nodded
earnestly, admiring the magical contraption. "He
looks so kind."

"The kindest. He lives on the farm where I grew
up. In a converted barn. By a brook. He used to
introduce himself by saying 'I'm Peter
Barnbrook, and I live in the Barn by the brook.'
Drove me crazy. Such a bad joke." We both
laughed heartily. "Sometimes having one amazing
parent makes up for the other being awful. My
mother was much like your Father. My father
made her promise to never return, after he
caught her hitting me, and for once, she stayed
true to her word. I'm so incredibly glad that the
universe chose my dad to be my dad. I'm
supposed to stay pretty detached from cases but...
Yours just hit so different. I went to make sure
your Mama was okay when you were in surgery.

She was just sat there crying, and she told me your whole story. Not as if she were reporting a crime or giving a statement. Like she was taking comfort in the heart of a dear friend. That night we spoke for hours, and hours, until her smile returned, and I can't look back. It's like I've known her my whole life." She blinked back tears and I saw a side of her I hadn't seen yet. A more emotional, fragile side, like that of an angel. Without a second thought, I wrapped my arms around her neck, and she held me back. "Thank you for saving us." I choked. "Sweetheart, you saved each other."

Suddenly, my mother appeared at the door with Bubbles, and another, white horse. She wore a smile of utter elation and spoke to them with a high pitched tone that anybody else would've mistaken as patronising. "Mary, that horse is trying to get into your house, honey!" Shonda exclaimed, jumping up and cackling. "They're going to help us get to the flower field!" My mum sung.

"Oh, you are such a beauty!" Shonda said, carefully approaching the animals and stroking their noses. While she held them, my mother came to me and guided me to Bubbles. She sat me on him and then jumped up in front, taking the reins with soft control. Shonda mounted the luscious white horse, that looked like a unicorn, minus the horn and wings, but was every bit as magical. Her name was Penelope. At a gentle trot, we made our way through the first field and lanes. I held onto my mother, so I didn't fall, leaned my head against her back, and closed my eyes. "Are you okay? Would you like to stop?" She asked anxiously, mid conversation with Shonda who was right beside us. "Not at all. I just finally feel safe enough to rest properly. I can smell the flowers." I whispered happily. "Me too. Me too."

The sun shone through the gaps within the trees and sliced through the dusty paths with admirable pride. As we approached the flower field I was shocked to find it even more beautiful than I had remembered it. Every flower waved to greet us in the wind. Mother nature's subtle perfume blessed our noses and reminded me of every smile I had ever smiled. The horses were weary with where they stood, careful not to trample as many flowers as possible as if they knew the secret of serenity the place carried. Its composure was one of genuine purity. I felt the presence of Darcy more than ever. The wind was her whispering 'hello' to me. I could feel the presence of Rosie too. The scent of the happy grass as we dismounted our two beautifully gentle beasts, was like her comforting hand upon my shoulder that time Jordan had locked us in the cellar as a mean joke, when drunker than ever on straight whiskey. I regretted our clashes and my unrepairable hatred I had felt for her before. I should have been more empathetic and taken time to realise the broken, scared woman she was, hiding in my father's grim shadows for protection. I didn't feel any of that in the flower field. All of my 'It's not fair that Darcy is gone' had turned to 'How lucky I am to be privileged to have loved so ridiculously deeply.'

I looked over at Shonda. "I feel as if I have been here before, but never before in this life." She said, composing each word with special care. "It has that effect on people." My mother said, holding me close as we walked to the centre where a patch of grass was left, untouched by the flowers. A perfect bed in the wild. Mama let the

The Field Where All The Flowers Grow

horses lie down and then sat beside Bubbles. I
joined her and she instinctively began putting little
braids in the front of my hair. It was golden hour
now, and dandelion seeds fell all around. When I
was little, I would wish upon them, but I didn't
need to now. There was no fear of loosing all I
had, just an immense gratitude that I had it. Each
seed that floated, was turned gold by the suns first
breath into the other side of the world's
tomorrow. Birds flew overhead, tweeting and
chirping and chasing each other with a harmless
competitiveness. For every note they sung, I
noticed something new and beautiful about my
surroundings. My mum wore a pale yellow
ribbon in her hair, that connotated such mellow,
calm, joy. I could have traced her smile to the
smallest detail as easily as I could write my own
name. The other two were talking fondly to each
other, about what, I didn't know. I couldn't hear
them. I could see their mouths moving and sense
the honied tones of their voices, but the words
were the least of my priorities. There was a silky
secrecy to us being here. Silky for sacred, and the
feel of the grass with which I was fiddling.

Above, the clouds spread and parted, and I half expected Darcy to reach her hand down and take us with her. She didn't, but she was certainly holding my heart. The petals of the poppies contrasted the opaque ones of the tulips. They flopped up and down, transparent to the light, but still red as the blood pumping life around my body. With each breath, a different floral scent became dominant as if they were playfighting for the prize of smelling the most beautiful. I thought that to be silly, as there would never be a clear winner. Lavender. Rose. Thyme. Lilies.

"Mum?"

"Yes, sweet thing?"

"How did all the flowers get here?" I asked curiously. "You know, I am so glad you asked. Your Grandma Julie's Father owned this land his whole life. His name was John, and he planted all of these incredible flowers as a gift to his wife; my grandmother. Lillian Grace. Hence all the lilies." She smiled to herself. "I used to come here with her almost every day. When she passed, she gave it all to me, and apart from you, it's truly the best gift I have ever received." She was now inserting small flowers into the gaps in my braids. "That's an incredible story, Mary." Shonda admired with a heart warmed, astonished gasp. "Right? You have her eyes. You have my eyes." My mother stroked my cheek as if to wipe a tear that wasn't there. When she had finished putting the flowers in my hair, I laid beside her and closed my eyes, allowing the heat to warm me into unconsciousness.

Chapter seven –

The next morning I awoke in my bed, which I had only slept in one other time. It was raining, as displayed by the window above the window seat. I got out of bed and dressed into one of the dresses I had packed what now seemed like a lifetime ago. I stared into the mirror and found my hair still intact from the previous night. I looked more lively, and my gunshot wound was so much better than before. I was now better able to notice the aesthetic interior design of the home. The hallway was lined with photographs of my mother all throughout her life. Some of the people stood frozen in time were unrecognisable, and a stroke of excitement spilt around my veins as I thought of my mum telling me who they were, and all the stories she could remember that came along with them. The last frame before the stairs contained a picture of Mama, Maria, and a child, perhaps two years old. Me. We were at some sort of funfair, and had our faces painted with little rainbows. I was sat on Maria's lap, and her and my mother held one of my tiny hands each. I could almost smell the hot sugar donuts through the glass frame. At the foot of the stairs, lay a large rug of wine-red and cream. Small tables were dotted around frequently, and each and everyone carried a white, glossy vase that flourished with marron and white flowers. The light wood floors were spick and span. Not a mess in sight.

As I entered the living room, I found it to be empty – so I searched for my mother elsewhere. On my hunt, I found a laundry room that smelt like the word cleanliness, and an office room where everything was in its place. It was then I came across my favourite person to ever exist, stood alone, painting on a big canvas. I watched her for a while, observing the tranquillity in which she devised colours I had never seen before, right before my eyes. Each brushstroke a work of art. Each flick of the wrist a miracle. She was painting us both, lying down in the field. Hands clasped. Eyes gazing into one another's. Strands of hair spread onto the grass and intertwining accidentally. I trod slowly, until I reached closer. The smell of paint smelt like the sound of my favourite song. Sheets sprawled on the floor, offering their service to this masterpiece, and catching any splash of lightly coloured water or tear of paint that dared to leave the perfection it was born into. Around, on easels were other half painted canvases and sketch books. It seemed as if my mama was constantly carried away with new ideas, so much so that she forgot about all previous ones. The windows in this room were covered by a layer of thin curtain, of a light beige colour, and a thin white netting that stopped minibeast and bugs from intruding. "You paint." I stated, pointlessly. "I do." She smiled that smile again, turning to face me. "You're the best. These all look so real and magical." I said, hugging her from behind. She kissed me on the face, her hands scored with streaks of stray paint. "Shonda and I had an idea while you were sleeping so cutely in the field, last night." She whispered excitedly. "You did?" She hummed and nodded before leaving her stool and walking to the stand alone sink in the corner, where she washed her hands with warm soapy water, letting foam creep up her arms to her elbows. "Are you going to elaborate?" I asked, innocently, extremely interested. "Well... We thought we could set up a charity. To help other people in our situation. Create a number they can call for help. In a safe way. Shonda is trained as a police officer, and we can join with the local authorities to take down anybody before anything gets as scary as it did for us. We can offer comfort and advice, and... Baby we can save lives." Stunned by this woman's inconceivable heart, I froze. "If that scares you, Shonda is happy to start it alone, and I am ever so happy to just watch from a far, knowing we made a difference." She said, placing both dried hands on my shoulders. "How soon can we start it?" She lifted me up in a huge hug and then we both started laughing and crying in sensitive harmony. Happiness painted the room almost as beautifully as my mama had painted those canvases.

That day, after her shift, Shonda brung her Father, and two of her colleagues that volunteered to help launch our newly born idea, to our home for dinner. "Hello Mr Barnbrook, it's so lovely to meet you!" My mother exclaimed, hugging him as if she had known him forever. "Hello dear, my goodness, it smells wonderful in here! Thank you for having us!" He replied back with a wholesome voice that carried years of knowledge and respect, all of which I wanted him to teach me in an instant. He wore a long-ish coat and a generic Grandfather hat. "You must be

Journey!" The first colleague said charmingly. He
was a tall man in his thirties with startling blue
eyes and perfect dark hair. "I'm Elijah. You can
call me Eli if you want. This is Quin." He
gestured vaguely to the woman beside him. She
was kind of small, though not so small that you
would notice it as one of the first things you
would notice if you ever met her. First, you would
notice her green eyes that carried a look of casual
compassion. Like she understood everything she
set eyes on much deeper than anybody else.
Secondly, you would notice her hair. The colour
of crushed ginger. Not blonde, *or* red but
something in between the two. And thirdly, you
would notice her voice. Genuine and comforting
and familiar like the voice in your head that
reassures you when nobody else knows to try. A
little husky. A little dainty. I was drawn to her
from the start. She interested me in a way I had
never been interested in a person before. I
wanted her to tell me her story and listen to mine.

After welcoming our guests, we all headed into
the living room, where my mother served a
spectacular evening tea, that she had magicked up
whilst I read to her, from the diary, that had been

the catalyst for all of this. Crumbling scones, home made jams, salads, sandwiches, fresh meats and cheeses and crackers and fruit, all blessed the table. We sat on the sofas and immediately started forming ideas for our new masterpiece. It was agreed that we would call the foundation 'Mary's Journey' which was hugely flattering. The idea was that we would have a phone number that anyone in danger of abuse or domestic violence could call, where we could offer advice, comfort, and send in for a rescue if required. If the caller needed discreet help, one of us would be sent to them, and asked to play the part of an old friend, or co-worker or delivery driver, and offer a safe escape before calling in backup to arrest the suspected abuser. On the phone, victims could use code words, or pretend they were talking to somebody they knew, if their abuser is nearby, to reduce any suspicion they may have. I truly felt such honour to be included, and the excitement that I might be able to help save even one person, disregarded the fear that accompanied it.

After hours of planning and preparation, the serious chatter turned to thrilled laughter. "Why did you become a policewoman?" I asked Quin

while the others were discussing. "My older brother was one. I liked to copy him with everything. He was shot on the job trying to save a little girl from a kidnapping. Seven years ago. And I swore from that moment on I'd continue his legacy." Her eyes told me she was delighting in the memory of her heroic brother. "What do you want to do as a career?" Without skipping a beat. "I want to write. Stories. I want- I need to be an author." I smiled, slightly embarrassed. "I know it doesn't save lives but-"
"It might. If you write about the right things. The right people. You can show people what to do, and what not to do without them even realising it. Not all superheroes wear badges, darling." There was an eruption of belly laughs, and we were both sucked back into the room.

That evening was a blessing, and after Shonda, Peter, Elijah, and Quin had left, my mother and I went to sleep with light, happy hearts.

"I would love to take you shopping this afternoon. Will you please let me take you shopping, beauty?" My mother insisted over breakfast that morning. "We can pick up your Grandmother and head into town. You only packed a few outfits, and I'd love to spoil you. I suppose you never received any of my birthday or Christmas gifts?" A note of sadness threatened her merry tone. My heart plummeted, and it showed on my face, evidently. "It's okay. That's okay. We have each other now. Nobody can get in our way now. Never again. I won't let them. You know I won't let them, don't you?" I nodded and swirled my fruit loops around in the bowl, their hued colours morphing into an unappetizing brown. I set down my spoon, now nauseated by the memory of living in that empty shell, with Jordan and my stepmother. "Are you alright?" My genial Mother asked, frowning, and tilting her head slightly, pushing a glass of water towards me. "What did they do with Rosie, Mama?" She leaned against the countertop behind her, and the rims of my vision hazed, grey and fuzzy. "They took her home and her parents cremated her like she wanted. Is there anything else you would like to know? It's really okay to ask questions." She looked pitiful, but not in a demeaning way. "Do you think they'll ever find Helen?" Silence. "I'm not sure. They're looking. A lot of people are looking. And... I will be informed the second anything comes to light."

"Are they going to try and take me away from you because you didn't tell anybody about what happened to Maria? Isn't that illegal? I know why you couldn't say, but what if they don't believe you? Where am I supposed to go?"

"Sweetheart." She walked over to me, turned my stool to face her, and then she put her face close to mine like a puppy showing affection. "I will not let anybody take you away from me. I don't imagine it will even come into the picture. Our Maria was completely alone after her Mama passed away just a few months before she did. I was all she had; nobody cared she existed accept my mother, who was also threatened to secrecy. At most they might question us and look in the house, but once they see how perfect we are together, they won't want to lay a finger on us. Alright? I promise. I promise." She squeezed my hand three times. I. Love. You.

When we pulled up outside, mystical Grandmother Julie's home, I realised I had never seen it from the outside. It was far more intimate than our home, and though she lived alone, it didn't look empty in the slightest. She closed the door, and then turned to us, stopping to sigh with

one hand on her heart as if she were trying to breathe in everything about this moment. She wore a large, brimmed hat that matched her shamrock green dress, as the ribbon that tied around it was white with a leafy green print, drawn with gold edging. "You look extraordinarily wonderful." I said, as she climbed into the front seat with Mum.
"Thank you princess! I am so happy to see you both!" She kissed my mother on the cheek, and reached her hand back, so she held mine for a moment. *My* mama enlightened *her* Mama on our foundation plan, and I observed carefully as her eyes began to glow with pride. "You surprise me every day, Mary. This is just wonderful. The world needs this. The world needs you."

The only malls I had seen before were the two local to our town in England. Small and sad. But this mall looked like something out of a Hollywood movie. My mouth hung open in astonishment, which made my mama and Grandmother laugh, tremendously. "What is so great about it?" Julie asked, chuckling still. "It's so clean and bright and there are so many flashy lights and fountains! Our mall at home was tiny

and sort of dingy in comparison." I admitted. My mother linked both of our arms and walked us up to the fountain. "Let's make a wish," She decided, scrambling in her pockets for spare coins. She handed us one each, and we tossed it into the water that looked a dazzling blue, thanks to the reflection of the painted concrete underneath. All at once, the three pennies broke the surface of the water and thrust drops of it upwards. I watched as they shifted other pennies on the bottom and hoped that the disturbance wouldn't affect other peoples wishes. "What did you wish for?" Mama asked curiously.
"I can't tell you. Or it won't come true." I said, seriously. She laughed again.

I never told her what I wished for, but I can tell you. I wished that no matter what, we stayed together forever. And not the forever scrawled in pink gel pen on the back of a birthday card written at eleven years old. Or the promise in a locket from a first love. Real, forever. As in, eternity. Unbreakable, inevitable, always, eternity.

Adorably, my mother brought us each a matching scarf. They were an awe inspiring lavender colour with golden butterflies sewn on in a specific formation. Each one in its place. She also brought me an entire wardrobe worth of new clothes. Dresses, two piece sets, shorts, jeans, skirts, tops, and jumpers galore.

We stopped for a coffee in a little indie café, with a bohemian style interior design. Wooden panels struck up the wall and onto the ceiling in cool patterns, and crochet tapestries hung, accompanied by strings of wooden and clay beads. It smelled of pine, courtesy of the mini trees in big brassy pots, and earthy, good, rich coffee beans. My mother ordered her and Julie a vanilla beam latte, and me, a chocolate frappe. I took the dome lid off the cup, and started licking the fluffy, glossy whipped cream off of the straw. The tiny fragments of ice melted as they touched my tongue, and I was enlivened by the deep chocolatey taste.

In the furthest booth, sat a woman with thin wiry lips and thick, straight, bristly, dark hair. She stared at me for a while, pulled out her phone, and started taking photographs of us. "Mum?" She stopped her conversation with her own immediately. "What's wrong? Are you all right?" I moved behind her and she held my cheek in her hand. "That lady is taking photographs of us. She knows who we are. How does she know?" I demanded, breathlessly.

"Okay. Okay. I'll oversee this." She stood up and walked over to the woman. "Excuse me, why are you taking pictures of my daughter?" She looked taken a back and gave her a very rude expression. "I'm a journalist. We're dying to know more of your story. How is she doing?"

"Please leave us alone. We've been through enough, please stop."

"Do you refuse to answer *her* questions too? She must have many." My mother swiftly turned, stormed over to us, gathered me and our bags up, and led me outside, with my grandmother following closely. "They must have seen us outside the hospital. There were press. So many people witnessed Helen taking you. I'm so sorry this is happening. I wish I could make it stop-" We were now outside in the car park.

Swarms of people, mostly dressed in black and other dark colours, jumped at us through bushes and from behind cars, groping towards our faces with mics in their gluttonous hands. Some carried cameras that flashed and blinded, while others yelled so much, the words being said all mushed into pointless, infuriating noise. "Mum!" I shrieked, as I was pulled from her. "STOP!" She launched at the people pushing between us. She tried to reach for my hand, but I was tripped up. Laughter erupted and echoed around as Julie started pushing people backwards, so my mum could help me up. My Grandmother looked almost comical, trying hard to stop these paparazzi gangs whilst insuring she didn't loose her hat. Finally, after stumbling and running, while trying to shield each other, we successfully got into the car. My mother had to beep the horn constantly to clear these zombie-like irritants from blocking our exit. Eventually, we lost them and drove home. I remained speechless in the back, while my two guardian angels muttered, enraged, all the way home.

Chapter eight –

The next weeks passed, almost smoothly. We visited the flower field so very often and made every second together count. We rode the horses, we baked, we cooked, we painted, and I read my stories to my mother while she sewed, or sculpted, or packed frames, and coasters, and pots, and canvases for orders. The evenings were made up of planning for the debut of 'The Mary's Journey foundation.' The table was always piled high with foods we had made in the daytime, and soon the others started to contribute. Shonda brought dishes of rice and pasta that her and Peter had made together, the thought of which was somehow even more heart-warming and delicious than the taste. Elijah brung bread rolls and vegetables that his Father had grown on their plot, not too far from our own land. Quin brought the good stuff. Chocolates, trifle, cakes, and puddings. Often, Quin would be the first to arrive, and she would come straight up to my room where she insisted I read her my latest poems and chapters. When I would read to her, she would sit on my bed and stare at me with huge, admiring eyes that flattered me endlessly. After, I would finish, and she would tell me the parts she liked the most. In a way, she reminded me a lot of Darcy, and I would take comfort in her a lot. She'd say, "What's up, missy?" And I'd simply tell her. No filter. And she always understood.

The night of a meeting, a few days after we had released the foundation's phone number, we overran and Quin stayed for the night, sleeping in the guest bedroom on the third floor, where Shonda and my grandmother stayed sometimes. In a deep sleep, I dreamed of Darcy and I playing the guitar together and singing, while she sipped cheerily on that all too familiar bottle of red wine. I could smell her. I reached out and felt her silky hair. "You have to go now, baby. Go save her."

"What? Save who?"

"Go! Go!" She dropped the guitar, and the strings gave a pained, jumbled cry. I awoke, gasping for air, to find Quiney at the door. "Wake up missy, we got our first call!" I sat up clumsily. "Are you okay?" She came and sat roughly on my bed, not caring as she messed up the covers. "It was just a dream. Darcy again?" I nodded and she laid, propped up on one arm. "I saved two halves of that cream cake downstairs for you. Why don't

we go downstairs, see who we gotta go save, and
have a cheeky breakfast?" I raised an eyebrow at
her. "What?" She scoffed, defensively. "You
can't have two halves of something, silly.
Otherwise it'd be a whole, wouldn't it?" She
creased and I giggled. "Smart ass."
"I'm not a smart ass. You're just stupid." She
pushed me lovingly, and I reluctantly left the
warmth of my bed, following her downstairs to
find everybody huddled together.

It was dawn and chilly. "Okay, everyone is here.
The caller is a nineteen year old female. Miss
Katy Lindley lives with an abusive boyfriend
against her will. Journey, this one is for you.
You're now nineteen year old Olivia Crane, and
one of Katy's work friends. We will be
surrounding the building; you need us, you just
shout. Try and stay on the down low, and just get
Katy out of the house." Shonda instructed slowly,
so I took in every word. This was all happening
so fast; I hadn't even been awake for five minutes.
"You can opt out sweetie, Quin can go if you're
scared." My mother said, coming out from
behind Elijah. "No. I've got this. I'll just get
dressed." She nodded and I raced upstairs, not

The Field Where All The Flowers Grow

willing to let Katy Lindley sit in despair for a
fraction of a second longer than she had to. I had
also become protective over Quin and would
rather I be the one to step into the probably
dangerous situation. I fumbled around in my
drawers and pulled out a pair of blue jeans, and a
stripey jumper, thrust them on, and ran back
downstairs. We rode in three separate cars, in
pairs, so we wouldn't look suspicious, all pulling
up down the road from where Katy lived. I of
course, rode with my mother.

"Okay, so number seventeen... Can you
remember that? Number seventeen- Are you
scared brave one?" She asked, looking over
briefly and almost forgetting she was at the wheel.
"I'm not brave. I'm terrified." I admitted, shakily.
"Bravery isn't having zero fear. It's having fear
and giving it a go anyway. You can turn back at
any moment. We can do this without you. I'm
not even truly happy about you doing this part.
I'd much prefer you to design the logo and
promote online and design the website, where I
can see you and know you're safe. But I won't get
in the way of your choice." Her voice wavered.
"I'll be careful. I promise. It's safe with you all

here. Terrible things can happen to anybody at any time. We can't let fear get in the way of success. Think how great we'll feel once we save Miss Lindley. Right?" I reassured her and simultaneously reassured myself, now ready and energised.

The clouds hung daintily in the sky, radiating dusty blues, greys, and pinks in whisps and swirls. The morning air was cold, and biting, and I felt nauseated with nerves, as if I was on some sort of roller coaster headed for hell. We pulled up. "I love you more than anything I have - or will ever know." Mama said, passionately. "Me too. I'll see you in a jiffy."
"A what?"
"A jiffy... As in... I'll see you in a second?" She looked puzzled, and then we both laughed. The laugh then turned into a cry, and we held each other close for a moment. She squeezed my hand three times again. "I'll be ten steps behind you. You can do this, angel." I nodded and turned, walking gingerly towards the house. What I saw when I arrived, shocked me to the core.

Discoloured, stained walls, trying desperately to look like a home, leaned uncertainly before me,

most of the windows barricaded and smashed.
Rubbish bags sprawled on the floor, ripped, and
vomiting mould onto the pavements that were
also showered with fragments of crushed, sharp
glass and what looked like potato crisps. Thick,
course, weeds sprouted from the front lawn, and
I noticed a single dandelion hiding between some
leaves. Instinctively, I reached down to pick it,
took it to my lips and blew, making a wish. A wish
that this would all go smoothly... and then, I
knocked on the door.

In the seconds it took for the door to be opened,
I endured a short lived, but very real, panic. More
than anybody, I was brutally aware of how quickly
lives could change, and end. I turned once to see
the lady ten steps behind me standing still and
was reminded of how quickly she had flown over
the boundary of lost forever and completely in
reach. In an instant.

A large, gruff, dirty man answered. "Who the hell
are you?" Unpleasant smells radiated from the
hallway, and I swore I saw a rat scuttle across the
floor. Spider webs clung to every nook and
cranny visible. "I'm Olivia. Katy's friend from
work. I was wondering if she wanted to come and

have lunch at my mother's house?" He looked behind him several times during that single sentence. "Come in." He grunted, placing an unconsented hand on my shoulder, tightly, and though I couldn't see her face, I knew Mama was already in protective mode, the second that psycho laid a finger on me.

When the door closed, barely any light existed. "Wait here." I nodded obediently and stood alone. The thunderous thud of his footsteps made dust scatter from the ceiling and unknown liquids dripped down the walls as if they too, were crying for help. A door swung open. "There's an Olivia downstairs. In *my* house. Says she wants you for lunch. Be back in two hours... Or I'll kill you." The man's voice was hushed, but I think he wanted me to hear him, because I did. A very thin woman, wearing ripped tights, a leather skirt and grey hoody ran down the stairs. "Hey, Liv. Thanks for coming." She breathed, shoving a pair of boots on her feet, and then gesturing we leave immediately. "No problem. My mum is just down the road." She smiled and we left, walking silently until I reached my mother and Peter at the end of the road. Sirens blared inconsiderately, like the sound of sheep being slaughtered, and I flinched into Mama's arms. She held onto me. "Good job, baby. Good job. Come on, let's go." She took my hand and then Katy's, and we rushed into the car. As we drove away, to the police station to drop Katy off, I saw Elijah, Quinney and a few other police officers break down the door and rush inside. Before she ran inside, Quin caught my eye and blew a little kiss. I pressed my hand up to the window and pretended to catch it.

"Thank you, thank you so much!" Katy gloated, crying, hysterically. "What you guys are doing is the most amazing thing in the world. I never would have been able to escape if the cops had just rocked up. And anyone who knows me, would never come, and make any excuse for me to get out, because they're all to scared. Thank you. Thank God for you."

What we had managed to do in the space of five minutes, changed somebody's always. I held that very close to me for all the days after that one and never let myself forget it.

That was the first of many rescues. But one of the only we were directly involved in. Because in just a month, our world would be smacked upside down again, and we'd have to rearrange our lives in ways we never could have imagined.

One night, a month or so after the rescue of Katy Lindley, my mother and I, ate dinner together in the dining room. Outside, the world was dark, but we were inside, safe from it. "Do you think Katy Lindley is okay?" I asked, finishing my pasta, and setting my cutlery side by side on the cleared plate. "I hope so. She's definitely better than when we found her. Thanks to you! Oh you were spectacular. I'm still so proud. I know I keep saying it but it's so very true. I got a sweet message from Quin saying the same thing last week."

"You did?" I asked, trying to cover the glow of happiness those words lit within my smile. "I did. She's coming round Tomorrow, to keep you company."

"Why? Where are you going?" The furthest she had been from me since we had reunited from our chaotic car chase incident, was a few yards. "I just have to go down to the courts and meet with

our lawyer. Don't threat, it won't take long. Promise." She took our dishes out into the kitchen. I followed her. "Will you see him? I want to come with you. It isn't safe."
"I won't see him. He won't be in the same building, let alone room. I promise, it will all be fine. It's late. You need rest. Now." Her unusually quickly paced speaking set me on edge, and she wiped her mouth with the back of her hand, then corrected her posture before giving me a strange, strained, smile. "Let me do the dishes." I insisted, walking forward. She blocked me. I took a step back. "I've got it. You go to sleep now." I looked down at the floor.
"Goodnight, Mama."
"Yeah. Goodnight, sweetheart. I love you."
"I love you too."

I climbed the stairs and went right to my room, where I locked myself in, and laid on my bed, my mind a reel of constant memories. It took me forever to fall asleep, and when I awoke, my mother had left. A knock came at the door, but I didn't answer. "Are you awake? Missy? Because I feel like you're dead asleep." Quin spoke quietly, and I remained perfectly still so she wouldn't sense I was misleading her into the belief I truly was wiped out. When it was safe and she had gone, I silently stared at the open window until the icy winds rushing through it made me so cold, I couldn't lie there any longer. I changed into one of my new outfits; some light denim jeans and a simple black strap top, and then wandered downstairs to find Quinney lounging on the sofa as if it were her own.

"Hi darling! I love the jeans." The room looked even more gorgeous with her in it. "Was my mum okay? When she left?" I asked, feebly. "She was. Are *you*?" I sat beside her and looked up into her angelic eyes. "I don't know-" The sound of a car pulling up grounded me, and I ran outside to find my mama looking up at me with big, grateful eyes and a smile so wide it made me giggle. Outstretched arms reached towards me and pulled me in. "Hello, hello! Oh my goodness, what a wonderful welcome!" My mother gleamed, looking around us as if somebody else was with us, that Quin and I couldn't see. "Let's head inside and grab a bite to eat... Then why don't we visit Shonda? We should make her a cake, all three of us." She said, reaching for a newly arrived Quin and kissing her cheek. We bustled inside and got busy making Shonda's cake.

In all my life I never knew anybody more generous than Mary Elizabeth Pinnock. At any opportunity she saw to give a gift, a gift was given. She not only jumped to help others, but leapt and smiled all throughout, obliterating any opportunity for the person she was helping to feel bad, or inconvenient. Being in a room with her changed you, every time, and never once got old. I swore I left the room an inch taller every time she called my name in fierce love or hugged me and told me I didn't ever have to worry, because she would always keep me safe. Cosy, selfless and patient. The best Mother a girl could ask for. The best woman in existence. The best gift in the world.

Eggs were cracked, butter and sugar creamed, and flour folded. When baked, the cake was slightly overdone, as we had gotten carried away with playing with watercolour pastels on huge sheets of thick, durable, sweet smelling sketchbook paper. The wonky surface was not a fantastic base for the fresh fruit to stand on.

Raspberries rolled, strawberry slices slid, and the white chocolate drip pooled around the plate, but none of that mattered because we had the most fun making it. Quin had provoked a little flower fight, so streaks of the stuff smeared my cheek, forehead, and arms. Gently, I wiped it off with a damp flannel, in the bathroom attached to my bedroom. "Will you stay tonight?" I begged. "I love it when you're here." She hummed a euphonious tune and nodded. "Of course I will stay, missy." She sat on the edge of the bath and looked out of the open window serenely. A lilac butterfly drifted, dreamily through it, and perched on the white wicker laundry basket. "You're just like Darcy, it's a shame you never met, I think you would have loved her a lot."
"There's still hope. She might be alive; we don't know yet."
"You're kind for trying." I smiled. "But everybody knows she's gone. It's okay. She's okay. I know she's okay." The butterfly left, carried by the wind. Quinney reached for my hand. "I'll look after you until you see her again. I promise, I'll stay whenever you need me, and you can call at any time. We've got each other. We've got each other." I silently squeezed her hand

three times, leaned my head against her shoulder
and closed my eyes. I suddenly became aware of
how tired I was and felt as if I could rest. That
day however, had no such plan.

Due to a last minute change of plan, Shonda
came to our home and collected the cake. We
shared it and were each delighted to find out it
tasted way better than it actually looked. My
mama turned the radio on, and pulled out a
purple, leather chest, full to the brim of old
photographs. Pictures of her early years, and
Maria, and me as a baby. My ultrasound scans,
parties, and shopping dates with my sweet
Grandma Julie came to life vividly in my hands
the more I stared at the pieces of the past, frozen
and preserved safely for us to keep precious.
There wasn't a single photograph that didn't have
a scratch, or tear, or torn, discoloured edge, and I
could tell my mama looked at them every day.
"Oh! This is my favourite of Maria!" She scoffed,
thrusting a small polaroid in my face, eagerly. I
took it, and found twenty-one year old Maria in
the flower field wearing a white dress. She looked
as if she were a feature of the field. A part of it
that had always and would always remain in its

essence forever. "She's beautiful Mama. Tell me more about her." I insisted, handing her back the picture and moving closer so I could absorb everything about to pass through her ruby red lips. "This picture was taken when she returned from a long trip. Gosh, she was gone for months, and I missed her terribly. She adored you. The moment she discovered I was pregnant, she ran to the store, and we picked out almost your entire nursery. She just knew you were a girl. Actually, she named you. She used to read you this poem she wrote, especially for you. I don't remember too much of it now, but it was about how she knew someday you would go on a marvellous journey to strength and love and do great things. And oh, how she was right." She fumbled around and retrieved from the piles of papers, a sandy coloured piece of paper with scrawled handwriting all over it. "She wrote?" I asked, fully entrenched in the brief, little story. "She did. All the time. Songs, poems, novellas. She used to read to you, before I put you to bed. I was too worried to hold you and the book at the same time, in case you fell and got hurt. In fact, when she travelled, before this photo was taken, all I received from her were poems. That was before

you were born. Way before, actually."
"Do you have any of her stories left?" I asked,
hopeful. "This. This was my favourite little song.
She used to sing it all the time." She cleared her
throat and sung sweetly. "Through the wind,
you'll stand, through the rain, you'll stand,
because wherever you go, I promise I'll hold your
hand. There is nothing that you could ever do so
wrong to make me fall out of love with whoever
you're one day going to be, and I'll watch your
path, and your sweet journey." Shonda wiped a
tear from her eye and Quinney applauded. "I
wish I remembered her." I choked, my chest
feeling like something large was sat on it. "Me
too. But I know she's still watching us and rooting
for us-"

The radio had spoken unforgivable words, and
with those words, sucked every piece of joy from
the room like a hoover to dust. Pitiless, easy,
cruel. Rain began to plummet from the heavens
again, and a shadow splurged into every corner,
darkening the once untouchable love in the
room. I winced. My mother sighed. Quinney
gasped. Shonda cried. "Anyone who thinks they
have seen this man should report to the police

immediately. Convict of murder, kidnapping, and domestic abuse, Mr Jordan Hunt has evacuated Jail unaccompanied, and is a danger to others, having killed his last victim in front of his own daughter, and ex-wife just last month. Police are urging any members of the public with any information to come forwards."

"Mama?" She looked down at me and I felt like an infant. "I have a second home in Louisiana. He won't find you there. We can go. Now." Shonda shook, horrified. "Right. Yes. Yeah, we should go. We need to go. Baby, go grab as much as you can, and pack it all into the biggest bag you can find. Okay?" She was crying huge, silent tears.

This woman was yet again turning her entire life upside down to protect us from this monster. Forced to leave behind every memory, brick, and plank of wood in her rear-view mirror. "What about the horses?" I sobbed, holding her cardigan tight.

"I'll take care of them, missy. Elijah will take them to Mr Barnbrook's farm, don't worry. This will all go away soon; it'll all be over soon." She promised, prizing me away from my mum so she could help me pack. I shoved all of my clothes, notebooks, and pictures into some bags Quinney had found, and then we hauled them into the back of Shonda's big car.

"I will be waiting for you. I will be waiting." Quin whispered, hugging me so hard it hurt. She held my hand so tightly I thought it might break. "Come with us!" I cried, not bearing to let go as Shonda pulled me away. Surrounding me was this pressure, as if the atmosphere was grinding against itself, and the force was building up in my ears like a silent sound. I tried to shake it off, but it only wavered and then returned, so everything seemed as if it were happening underwater. "No! Quin!" I resisted Shonda's Motherly grip and broke free, racing back into Quin's arms. I felt like if I left her, she would get hurt and I would be responsible, just like I felt I was for Darcy. "Don't yell, missy. We're fine. It's just a little trip. I'll see you in a little while." She didn't sound convinced and wouldn't let go of my hand. "Keep writing. Write when you're lonely. Write when you're scared. Ok? Go. I'll be okay. You can go. You have to go."

I knew *she* would be okay. But what about me? I didn't know how I could cope, being far away from her for so long. All the air in the world couldn't satisfy my lungs. I couldn't breathe. Not in a classic, panicked way, but so badly I thought I might die, right there. My mama noticed and moved in front of me. "You can breathe. You can. I know you're scared. I'm scared too. Quin will be here when we return. We will return. Soon. Very soon. We might not even get to Louisiana. But right now, we need to go. We need to get as far away from here as possible. Do you understand?" I nodded and gave Quin one last hug. The saddened scent of my burning tears and her perfume made me feel ill. Then, I looked away and did the brave thing by leaping into the car. As ours drove into the night, I could make out the colours and shapes of another car making its way to our house. It was Elijah, on his way to collect Quinney. He would protect her. He would keep her safe.

I allowed my face to rest against the cool glass that sent a shiver through my whole body, and watched, as we drove away from our haven. Away from home. Away from the field, where all the flowers grew.

Chapter Nine –

My legs, back and neck ached horribly for the entire duration of the car ride, no matter how many times I shifted around or moved positioning. My bones felt like led, weak and bruised, and no matter how hard I fought, I couldn't fall asleep. And although I stayed conscious, I was barely present. My mother and Shonda were on the phone with the authorities every half an hour to update them, and to be updated themselves. From what I could make out, nobody had seen my father, though somebody local had reported seeing Helen, so I was glad we had left when we did.

Every car I saw on the way felt like it was her car. I was ready, at any point to fight for my life again, in a heartbeat. I had more to live for now. I had a true sense of purpose.

When we got to Shonda's second house I was startled at its beauty. Right next to the shore, it stood firmly with nothing around it. I walked up the path, hand in hand with my mama who was tiredly fumbling over her words, trying to compliment Shonda on how lovely everything looked. Panged with homesickness, I noted the yellow tulips lining the white picket fence. If

The Field Where All The Flowers Grow

Shonda was a house, this would be her. Fun and
joyous, chaos streamed and squiggled from all
around it. When walking through the front door,
we were dazzled by the funky, bright, patterned
wallpaper, the sight of which sat perfectly between
aweing and the vision disturbances that come with
a migraine. "I will go out to the store and pick up
some food for us. Are you okay to stay here?"
Shonda questioned, cautiously. "Yes, of course.
Thank you so much, my love." My mother
smiled. Shonda left almost immediately, leaving
us alone for the first time in a while.

"Let's sit." Mama took my hand as if it had
recently recovered from injury and led me to the
strikingly green sofa. For somebody who barely
lived there, Shonda kept many plants which were
all flourishing as if they paused living completely,
all the while she wasn't there. "I'm so glad you're
my mum." I said suddenly, as if I had an awful
case of word sickness. "I don't care that we had to
wait so long for this. I'd rather spend one day
with you in my whole life, than a lifetime with
anybody else."
"Oh, sweetheart. I feel the same way about you.
Exactly the same." I looked out of the window

facing Shonda's lawn. "He's going to find us," I whispered, as if Jordan was in the room. "He's going to find us; we aren't far away enough." My mother looked at me as if I had just told her I never wanted to see her again. "I thought I could keep you safe, but... I'm scared you're right. I'm doing everything I can, and I will continue to do just that. That's all we can do. All we can do is our best to protect each other. Whatever happens, we'll stay together." She pulled a crochet blanket from her bag and laid it over me. "Maria made this. She made it for me when I had you."

"It's so soft." I yawned, and laid down slightly.

"Soon, we'll be far away from here, sweet one. Somewhere warm, and kind, and full of life. We'll have a new house together in a place where nothing bad has ever happened to us. And we can paint it together. We can paint a new life for ourselves. Give a girl a paintbrush and she'll paint her own gorgeous, happy life, hey honey? Your Nana would love it out here. I'll get her to come. I'll call her. Just in case we're here a while." She giggled to herself and then sighed again, cuddling into me, and holding me until I felt safe enough to fall asleep.

The Field Where All The Flowers Grow

"We're so lucky. Oh my goodness, another one just came through for two hundred dollars. A Mr Kevin Harriet." Shonda's voice glowed in the darkness of my closed eyes, which I soon opened. Propping myself up on my arms, I saw the two angels surrounded by paperwork. "Hi baby. Come look at this!" Mama begged, reaching a strangely elated arm out. I wandered over and found a list of names. Katy Lindley's name sat on top of a list of about fifty. "This is a list of every person we have helped, or who has donated, or who works with us. This many, in the amount of time we have been open is incredible. Thousands of pounds worth of donations we can use to help victims without a home to go back to. We may have saved lives by just picking up the phone." I picked up the vast list, checking it was real and looked into Shonda's eyes, wistfully. "This is wonderful." Quickly, I set it down and rushed into the bathroom - not so fast that it was suspicious, but with enough speed, that nobody spotted the tears starting to flood my face.

Why was nobody here to save *us?* Selfish, I know, but that was all I could think. I fell to the tiled floor on my hands and knees and prayed silently. I moved my mouth with the words I wanted to say, but ensured I was silent, so nobody worried. I remember hushing sobs with both of my hands prized over my mouth. Sobs that made my whole body heave. This was all such a mess. I reached for some tissue that shredded and disintegrated at the touch of my acidic tears. They burned my skin and made my face all red and itchy, so I felt like I had rinsed it with stinging nettles. I slopped the useless, obliterated tissues into the bin, and dared to look into the mirror to find the reflection of the person whose fault this all was. I knew I had no control over being born, though I had this undeniable sense of guilt over the fact I was. Things might've turned out so differently for everybody else. I splashed handfuls of water on my face and watched as the red patches calmed. When I had waited out the puffy eyes and looked presentable, I made my way back into the room.

"Quinney just messaged me to say the horses are safe, and that she's going on a rescue today to help another lady."
"She's a hero. Like you two."
"And you. You did the first. You paved the way."

The Field Where All The Flowers Grow

That statement made my heart feel like a frustrated hand was clenching it tight, the same way Rosie would carelessly brush my hair with force if I had irritated her before or during my hair being done. I honestly wish I knew more about her. She was fairly plain from all I knew, but how much of her I knew I would never know. Now, try saying that fifty times in a row.

For two weeks, we lived a painfully boring, repetitive life. Wake up. Stay inside. Eat. Go back to sleep. We were all becoming increasingly hopeless and miserable. Julie was in hiding with the police and called us every day. I did my best to try and cheer up my own Mother because I knew how she missed hers, terribly.

If I could have gone back to those weeks and told myself anything, it would have been to make every moment count for something. Hug more, cry less, dance around even when people are watching. Think smarter not harder. Set your mind to something great and just do it because if you don't let anything stop you, it won't. Climb the hills, watch the sunsets, and smell the flowers.

Because when you come round and wish you had - it's almost always too late.

Blossom drifted like fresh, puffy flakes of snow and settled neatly into place on the grass, as shown by the window I could see from the bed. A knock softly came from the door, and I turned over, facing away from it. I had been lying there alone, thinking of Jordan finding us for hours. Shaking, cold, and terrified beyond compare. I felt like a small animal, defenceless and awaiting its inevitable doom. Behind me, I could hear the door open, and my mother entering the room. "I made us some tea." She admitted, her voice a little strangled. "S- Sweetheart. Journey?" She set a tray down on the drawers and crouched at my bedside. "What's up, buttercup?" She tried to smile and wiped some of the tears from my glassy eyes. "I feel like this is all because of me. I just want it all to end. I don't think this is something we will ever just get over. We can't be happy and live normal lives even if everything was to be resolved, right this second. I don't want it anymore. I don't- I wish it would all go away but it can't. It never will."
"You're right. This won't be something we can

just get over. You're right about that. But you're oh so wrong about the part where we won't ever be happy again. We will be happy one day. On a lot of days, actually. We will live long, satisfied, and peaceful lives together, until Maria and Darcy and Rosie and everybody up in the sky calls us home. Sweetheart, do you remember what I told you the first night you came back to me? About how when one door closes the whole world opens right up. That door is waiting for us to be ready. We might not even realise we've passed through it for a while when we do. We will dance. We will sing and cook and write. Many times. I can feel it. And most importantly... I need you to know that not one single iota of this... any of this, is your fault. Okay? Come here." She relit a little light within me with one of her iconic hugs and then sat on the bed beside me, where we drunk our tea. "Oh, Shonda has gone back to Texas, her Father came and picked her up this morning because she needs to go and do a rescue nobody could cover accept her. She was vague but it seemed urgent." Mama told me, as if she were trying to remember if Shonda had left anymore details. "Has Quinney messaged you much?" She asked after a pause. I shook my head. "Not at all.

By Felicity Jayne

I don't want to bother her."
"Oh, you could never. How would you feel about taking a little walk around? Not too far. I just think some fresh air could do us both some good."
"I would like that."

Cosily dressed, we headed outside and made our way down to the shore. The sand was fine and white like powdered sugar and a vast variety of shells and precious looking stones covered it. The water was so clear, and I longed for the ability to be able to swim with Mama far away to the place we dreamed of and spoke about so often. Perhaps we could grow a flower field of our own there. Watch it grow up as we grow old. I looked behind me often to check the house hadn't up and left us, which considering the year we had had, wouldn't have surprised me one bit. It was still there, however.

"Through the wind, you'll stand, through the rain, you'll stand, because wherever you go, I promise I'll hold your hand. There is nothing that you could ever do so wrong to make me fall out of love with whoever you're one day going to be, and I'll watch your path, and your sweet journey."

The Field Where All The Flowers Grow

My mother sung Maria's lullaby with a lyricalness to her voice as light as a feather. She sung it again. And again. I just looked up at her the whole time trying to comprehend how lucky I was to get to have her be my mother. But there she was, before me. Mine. And I, hers.

Mary Elizabeth Pinnock wasn't the only person from whom I received the gift of Motherly love, however. In my life, I was able to experience it in so many ways from so many different people. Of course, none of the others compared even slightly to the love I felt for, and from my mum, but there were others close. Weather it was Darcy packing me lunch notes when I was reluctant to go to school, or Rosie making herself late for work so she could curl my hair to make sure I was going to look pretty for school picture day. Granted, I was often left with bruises from her hitting me with the hairbrush, but only out of frustration – never malice. Some people just struggle with how to outlet their pain and feel the need to pass it onto others. I understood even further with Rosie because she never even wanted me in the first place. I was sort of the cost to her having Jordan.

I bet now; she'd choose me over him in a heartbeat.

Shonda also acted extremely maternally towards me. She made my favourite meals and taught me recipes she had learnt from her childhood, never failing to accompany the stories that came with each one. It truly takes a village. Mine just happened to be a rather dysfunctional village. But a village none the less.

The slushing of the waves fed a calmness into my veins, that I had not felt for what seemed like an eternity. It was growing colder, but I didn't mind much, until it began to look like rain was about to implode upon us. In the safety of Shonda's home we took another nap on the couches, awoken only by the awful cry of Mama's phone. Sleepily, she reached out for it and held it to her ear.

"Hello? Who is this, please?" Through my blurred vision I saw her face turn grey. "No- No! Please! Don't! No!"
"What? What's happening?" I screamed, shrilly, moving to the other sofa, and holding her firmly.
"I am giving you fifteen hours to get here, or I am killing them all. Every single one of them. If you

call the authorities or any of the people I have sat
here under my watch, they all die anyway. Then,
we come and find you. Do you understand?" It
was Helen, her voice crumbling like slabs of
sharp rock breaking apart from its own cliff and
smashing into obliterated fragments on its way
down to the choppy, dizzying ocean. Jordan
could be heard yelling at the mystery people in
the room. "Come to me and I let them all go.
Every last one of them goes." I could have sworn
I heard Quinney cry so I instinctively threw up on
the floor beside me. "Okay, okay! I promise!" My
mama sobbed. Other, vague, unimportant words
were said and then the phone was hung up.
Mama pulled my hair back into a ponytail and
passed me some water. "Come on, baby. Are you
okay?"

How could I possibly have been okay? They had
Quinney. Helen was surely going to kill her and
whoever else was there. Then us.

"Are we going to die now? Are they going to kill
us?" I sighed, doubled over as my mother
hurried around, putting my coat on me so I
would be warm enough. "Not if I get there first.
I'm not a killer. I'm not. But I am a Mother, and

even the gentlest creature must turn to everything they've got to protect what's most important to them. And that. Is you. We need to get in the car right now. She says she's got every donor, victim, and worker of the Mary's Journey foundation in the attic of our home. Helen says if we get there late or try and do anything she will kill them all. And Jordan still wants to kill us. I thought it was so he could carry on living his life without having to be reminded of all he has done. But now I'm sure he's just a monster hung by the rope of his self-crafted origin story. He will receive no gain by killing anybody else. And he is not going to. I will make sure of that. In Shonda's car, she stores all of her spare police gear that they use for foundation rescues. Guns, pepper spray, tear gas. We're going to use it. Only what is necessary. We go in through the front, present ourselves as they wish us to, and then I will save us. You need to trust me. I'm not even quite so sure I trust myself right now... But will you please trust me? I need you to trust me, gorgeous one."

"What if it doesn't work? What if everybody- what if we all-"

"We won't. Don't think of it like that... Think of it like we're going home. Let's go home and see

Quinney." Earnestly, she hustled me out of the
house and right into Shonda's car, with a few
blankets and pillows. "I hope Shonda didn't go to
the house." I cried bitterly, terrified. "I know. Me
too. But I imagine she got the same call as us but
didn't want to take the risk of saying anything.
She's one of the bravest women I have ever
known, and I don't think for a second she would
have sat by and let anybody harm what we have
worked so incredibly hard to create."

As we left the house, it was sunset, and we drove
all through the night, our headlights slicing
proudly through the darkness like a beam of fake
hope. I counted the streetlamps on the
motorways, though lost count every ten or so,
because of how speedily we were soaring. At
several points I swore the tires lifted from the
ground. The moon apologetically froze in its
timid glow above us, while we spoke about the
future as if by talking about it, we were securing it.
"What colour do you want *your* bedroom to be?"
I asked my mama with a shiver. "Hmm. I have
always loved purple. A light, cheery purple on
one wall and white on the rest. Purple rug, white
furniture, and violet curtains." She smiled slightly

with the corner of her mouth. "Are you scared?" I asked quietly.

Silence stole the next few moments.

"Spend your life in a job you love. Whatever that may be. When you meet somebody and fall in love, tell them, and don't you ever waste a single second of time with them. And when you have a baby, don't feel pressured to name her after me. Name her something that feels right. Something pretty, and strong. Raise your children to be kind, like their gorgeous Mama; and if you ever miss me, look into your heart and I promise I will always be there. You won't hear my voice, but I'll be listening. And keep me alive in the stories you tell to the people around you. Stay with Shonda. She'll be a fantastic Mother to you-"
"Mum- Stop it! Shh! I don't- Just stop!" She laughed slightly hysterically and then wiped her eyes free of tears. "Just in case. Just in case." She coughed, discreetly attempting to catch her breath. "I don't want you to talk to me like that. I hate it." I snapped, flinching away from her as if her grieving eyes had the power to turn me to stone. "I love you. I love you."

The Field Where All The Flowers Grow

"I love you more."
"That's impossible."

On the thirteenth hour of driving toward hell, we arrived. The dusky polaroid-like film that coated my vision of the house and everything around it, made every bit seem more nightmarish. The car groaned and screeched in pain as we dragged it mercilessly across the sharp, jagged, rocky path. Nothing could have prepared me for seeing Jordan's face for the first time since he had savagely murdered Rosie and shot me in the hip. Ghostly and barely present, his face illuminated the window with a dauntingly sinister glare. "I have the gun hidden. But I've got it. Don't say a word, just stay close to me. Alright?"
"Okay. Nobody ever loved you as much as I do." I said, from an unspoken place, very far away. Once more, she wrapped her arms around my body and kissed my forehead. This was it – wasn't it? I was sure. I knew. This was it.

Chapter ten –

Your heart keeps you alive. That's no secret. It pumps blood around your body and beats in a rhythm that depends on how you're feeling, where you are and what is happening in that moment. Your heart races fast when you're afraid. Your heart beats slower when you're calm, relaxed and happy. Sometimes it flurries or skips a beat if you've seen something truly exhilarating. And your heart stops, usually only once. When you die.

Nothing could be heard accept our footsteps on the gravel. I focused intently on how the sound changed as we walked from stones, to wood, to kitchen tile. I looked left, then right, like I was taught to when crossing the road, as a child. Once, for a road safety awareness day, we were all herded onto a buss and driven to a field where emergency service businesses set up tents and showed us pictures that I could still recall in scarily, gross detail. With the pictures, came stories in attempt to scare us into being safe. I didn't need any pictures or stories to scare me into being careful now. I just had to be.

The Field Where All The Flowers Grow

The coast seemed weirdly clear. No guns. No
Jordan. No Helen. A huge sigh of relief. And
then another step forward. I stayed very close to
my mother and made sure that one point of my
body was always attached to hers, so it knew she
was still with me. A few plates, burdened with old
food from the day we had left the once
miraculous cookie dough smelling kitchen, could
be seen rotting in their own stench. Flies buzzed
around with zero coordination, and I flinched as
one's wing zipped my cheek. Slowly and steadily
we reached the foot of the staircase. Staring up at
it, it looked as if it would never end, and I
wondered briefly if that was a foreshadowing and
perhaps we would never even make it to the top.

Mama hadn't looked at me since we had entered
the building. Not until this point. She nodded
once and then held my hand firmly and
protectively, as we walked towards the attic.

The shallow shells of the rooms had been mined
of all their good memories, and it felt as if the
bricks and wood it was devised of, had never
heard a single laugh or seen a single smile in the
entirety of existence. The remaining photo
frames on the wall were smashed and spat glass

onto the stairs. Then the ladder. First went my mother and I followed, crying silently now as our faces, then necks, then arms, and so on, emerged into the dank, dusty attic. I could see nobody in sight, and I could tell my mother couldn't either, from the expression on her face as she used one arm to hook me closer to herself.

"Don't be afraid. Don't be scared. Honey, it's me-" Wide eyed I stared at my mother. Darcy. It was without a shadow of a doubt, Darcy's voice. I'm astonished my neck didn't break with force as I twirled around, desperate to see her perfect face. And then, from the depths of the shadows, sprung Helen, and Jordan. He carried a smile that dreuled with satisfaction and she... She carried a voice tape and pressed the button on it. "Don't be afraid. Don't be scared. Honey, it's me." Not Darcy, but an old recording of her voice.

As I looked up into my mother's exceedingly kind eyes, I saw for the first time ever, a tidal wave of explicit rage. 'Come on. Just pull out the gun so we can run, Mum', I thought, as my skin started to burn again. "Where are they?" She bit through gritted teeth. "Wine cellar." Hellen laughed wildly, like a cartoon witch. "Well, we're here. What do you want?" My mother pleaded. "I think you know." Jordan smirked. I suddenly had an idea.

"Daddy, please don't hurt us." I frowned, blinking back tears of distress. He jumped and then looked at me as if he had only just remembered I existed. "I have to. You both made such a fool out of me. Especially *you.*" He turned his nose up at Mama as if she were something unpleasant on the bottom of his shoe, that no matter how hard he tried to scrape off, remained insistent on sticking.

"There's no way I was having my baby raised around you and that woman. What was her name? Martha?"
"Don't you speak of her. I'll kill you! And you know her name was Maria; you piece of shit." All at once my mama and Jordan pulled out their guns and pointed them at each other's faces. "Daddy, NO!" I screamed as Helen wrenched me backwards roughly. "Why are you doing this?"
"Because of what your Mother did to me! Her and that woman were planning to take you away.

I loved her. But I had to fight for her love. You just got it. And so did Maria." He spat on the floor as if he were repulsed by the thought of her. "So I took you for myself and allowed her to communicate with you, but even without knowing who she was, you both loved each other more than you ever loved me. You ruined everything. Your presence destroyed my life. It killed my baby sister. She knew what happened to Maria, and that would never have happened if she hadn't tried to take you back from me. I just wanted them to learn a lesson. But when everything went down I knew what I would have to do. It just took me so damn long to bring myself to do it. I didn't want my Darcy to live scared forever. I did her a favour." I struggled, but Helen held me in a solid grip. "What will killing us solve?" I breathed, viciously.

"It will soothe the humiliation fraught on me by you both. There's no turning back for us, so we might as well get something good out of it." He growled, exchanging glances with Helen.

A shot. Through the latch door, Quinney had shot at Jordan, forcing him to drop the gun which slid across the room. Blood sprouted from his leg, and he used his hands to plug the wound. Helen, defenceless, released me and I ran back behind my mother, who had picked up the other gun. Just as I thought we were safe, Helen launched at us, clawing at my clothes, ripping my skin from my shoulder, before my mama could hurry me out of the door. When she had done so, both guns still in hand, she, Quin, and I raced from the landing, and down the stairs. My legs hardly worked now, but we all dragged each other forwards, refusing to let a single one of us fall behind. "Is he lying about having everyone in the wine cellar?" I gasped, clinging to Quin, and gagging on big, choked sobs. "Yes, sweetie, everybody is fine. Shonda came back the second we knew what Jordan was doing. Elijah spotted him in a back alley buying a gun off somebody when he was on a rescue. Crazy timing. We called Shonda and all waited around the house, using you as the bait." We were outside now. Shonda came onto the radio and her voice was the first thing that made it feel possible for me to get out of this alive. My mama was silent and grave. "Quinney, love, get them to the flower field, we need the area cleared for when they come out of the house, okay?"

"Okay." We pelted along the country lanes, through mud as thick as chocolate frosting, and had our hair whipped thoroughly by the fresh wind around us.

My mother was the first to climb the gate into the flower field but I, passed over by Quinney, followed very closely behind. As soon as I hit the grass, so hydrated with green, I felt like I was being hugged. Had we got out? Had we escaped? We made our way to the middle of the field and got down low, laying within the wise roots, dancing petals, and proud stems. The dew glistened, and soaked us, cooling us down. "You did it, Mama." I whispered, proudly. "We can go to the place we imagined now. Me and you." She held my hand and cried into my shoulder. I stroked her hair, feeling the purity of the gold locks on my trembling fingers. Though that, as I think you have probably come to expect, was too good to be true.

A fierce, calculated rustle, thrashed through the grass, and as I dared to move, I saw Helen storming towards us, a new gun, aimed. Without a word, she shot me in the stomach. I felt the bullet penetrate my skin, flesh and then liver, with

its agonising intention of killing me. "NO!" My
mother screeched in a way only a parent is
capable of screeching when their baby is hurting.
The fact she sounded so pained, pained me far
more than any bullet ever could. "YOU DON'T
GET TO BE WITH HER! *I* SHOULD HAVE
HAD MY MUM – NOT HER!" Helen
screamed, collapsing to the floor, gun still
pointed. "YOU DON'T EVEN RECOGNISE
ME! DO YOU? DO YOU? DO I NOT LOOK
ENOUGH LIKE HER, MARY?"
"I don't know who you are!" My mother yelled,
defensively. "YES! YOU DO! I'm... I'm the love
child! Remember that year when your beloved
Maria went to travel for six months? Me! She had
me! I am Maria and Jordan's daughter! I was
given up for adoption the second I was born
because she never wanted children. I reached out
and found Daddy a few years ago. He told me
how Maria threw me out and then practically
raised a daughter with you, fifteen years later!
Never once did she EVER make ANY effort to
contact me. I was old news; she wanted the new,
shiny toy!" I was shot again, but then Quinney
shot Helen right between the eyes. My sister laid
down to rest, and never moved again.

By Felicity Jayne

"Mama? I'm scared. I don't want to die. Doesn't the world know I don't want to die? I want to stay with you." A look I had never seen before came across her face. So, wrapped in fury, my mother got to her feet and cried out at the universe. As her voice soared high and whacked the skies, they split, shattering lightning down to earth, and pelting another set of raindrops on us. Quinney held her hands over the holes in my stomach and held me to her heart. "I feel dizzy. Everything's going darker." I sniffed, closing my eyes because keeping them open required a level of effort I just didn't have anymore. The usually strong and stable arms that were around me quaked and shivered. The usually smiling face above, grey and in mourning. "Mary, don't let me be the last person to hold her in their arms." Quin ordered, flinching as if I were made of something that was causing her pain, as she touched my cold, pale skin. "She's not dying! SHONDA, HELP! SHONDA!" Mama called, as if our lives depended on Shonda being present to witness my death. "MARY!" Quin screamed again, this time making my mother jump out of her skin. Immediately, she understood. If she wanted to

hold her baby again while she were still breathing,
now was the time.

The grass stroked my bare arms and legs, as I
died it maroon with my blood while Mama took
me into her trembling arms. Soon, the grass
would be yellow, and each blade split down the
middle, crumbling under the eternal stain of my
blood. "You stay with me. You stay. She stays
with me. " She prayed. The blue bells jingled
around in their jolly spirits and the roses flooded
my heart with their traditionally breath-taking
beauty, that stood even firmer among the grey
scene. "It doesn't hurt. I promise. It doesn't hurt
one bit." I wiped my mother's tears from her
face, though while doing so accidentally smeared
a little blood on her cheek. The smudge looked
oddly like a love heart with slightly unclear
margins. "It doesn't?" I shook my head and
forced a smile despite feeling more lost than I
had ever felt before.

You should know that Shonda continued growing
the 'Mary's Journey' foundation by watering it
with love and feeding it attention, every free
second she had. She gave advice to thousands of
women nationwide every year, and saved about

By Felicity Jayne

fifty lives with first hand rescues, annually.
Watching these scared souls turn into
independent, powerful individuals, was the most
rewarding thing in the entire world, and there was
nobody better suited for the job, than her.

Another smothering crash emblazoned the earth
with a vile shudder, and rain thrust upon us from
the crack in the aloof clouds. "Shonda is- Help is
coming, just hold on sweetheart, Mama's got you.
You're safe. You're okay." She sat me up against
her chest and I smoothed the ends of her now
soaked hair with my fingertips, as if they had
Rapunzel's magical healing powers, or something
of the sort. Quin turned away as if she couldn't
bear to see the end of my story and began talking
hurriedly into her phone, the words she was
saying just an irrelevant background murmur.
While she was turned, and I started to fall asleep,
my eyelids and every bone in my body felt
exhausted, like they had been replaced with
chunks of scolding acid.

Quin and Elijah fell madly in love and had an
intimate spring wedding in the flower field.
Chandeliers were hung from the oak trees leading
to the field, and the cake had fluffy, light pink,

rose frosting made by Grandma Julie. It was a spectacular scene, and me and Mama had the best seats in the house, as everybody rode the horses down natures holy isle, in white dresses, at sunset – their vowels spoken in the company of friendly croaking frogs, mini-beasts, fifty thousand flowers, and us. I'm sure the fireflies had some fantastic stories to buzz to their families as they flew home that night.

Two final shots. One. Two. The second from Quin's gun as she whipped around and plunged a bullet into Jordan's heart, from so far away. The first, from Jordans gun. Time slowed. My mother and I lay side by side among the sloshing, milky, frothy, filthy mud. Our hands clasped for eternity. Lightning whipped the sky. "Don't threat, strong one. I'm still here." Mama spoke, weakly.
"I'm still here too. Don't let go. I don't want you to let go of my hand." I sighed, sleepier by the moment. "Never, my baby. Never. I'm right behind you. I'm right behind you."

My incredible Grandmother Julie joined us soon after we ascended, if you're thinking about time on earth, time passes differently here. A whole life to you, as you read this, is but a mere second to us, leaving barely any time to miss anybody at all, yet all the time in the world to witness every step they take. So I urge you to look at this not as a tragic ending but one of immeasurable love and healing. In my short life I achieved far more than I ever imagined and met the most incredible people to ever exist. I saw, I listened, I heard, and I did. God, I'm so happy I did.

Your heart races fast when you're afraid. Your heart beats slower when you're calm, relaxed and happy. Sometimes it flurries or skips a beat if you've seen something truly exhilarating. And your heart stops, usually only once. When you die.

My mama squeezed my hand. Three times.

The rainfall hushed, and an overpowering warmth seeped through me, kindly. Butterscotch yellow, and arctic blue, whirled among splutters of rose and white whisps of clouds, in the sky. I noticed that the hand laid on my stomach was dry and clean, and I found myself able to lift my head up all on my own without an inch of, or any idea of what pain really was. My mother was awaking too, and the second her eyes clocked our blood-

The Field Where All The Flowers Grow

less clothes, sent a dazzling, sweet music right to my heart. Not a blade of the grass surrounding us was bent, or brown with filth from the storm, and a subtle tweet or two sounded from the trees around us.

Rainbow ombre petals, stuck on disks of fuzzy yellow, took my breath away, and I looked around, knowing at once where we were. I had been here before, though my previous visit was considered just a drop of water in an endless ocean. The air was warm and smelled like familiarity. In the distance, I saw two women in pearly white dresses that I recognised instantly. I looked up at the face of my mama now. She seemed to have figured it out long before I had. We were home.

The wind began singing and wafting leaves into a Romantic dance that glued themselves together with the binding force of pure, true love. From the leaves, green, rust, and fiery orange, formed a woman. Towards us she strode peacefully, with her hands held out as if to take ours. Then, she opened her mouth and drawn from those miracle lips, came the most indulgent sound known in that place, or any place for that matter.

"Through the wind, you'll stand, through the rain, you'll stand, because wherever you go I promise, I'll hold your hand. There is nothing that you could ever do so wrong to make me fall out of love with whoever you're one day going to be, and I'll watch your path, and your sweet journey."

Author Bio

Hoping to spread the importance of love, hope and gratitude, Felicity Jayne O'Toole (just seventeen years old,) devised her debut title, 'The Field Where All The Flowers Grow.' Felicity drew inspiration from a few of the many special, loving people in her life to create the sweet characters that you've hopefully grown to love.

Writing this sweet novella has given the seventeen year old a "much needed break from her school life!" Felicity says that she one day hopes to "be in a position where she can advocate for stopping bullying and generally making the world a kinder place."

The also aspiring actress says her "biggest dream is to see, 'The Field Where All The Flowers Grow' on the big screen where I would play protagonist 'Journey Hunt.' I drew a lot on my own characteristics when creating Journey and feel so connected with her."

By Felicity Jayne

The Inspiration behind 'The Field Where All The Flowers Grow' and its characters

Mary – I knew I wanted the heroic Mother of this story to have some connection to my own heroic Mother, who I am eternally grateful for, every day. When discussing the idea with her, she suggested the name 'Mary,' as it is her Mother's (and my wonderful Nan's) middle name and was also her amazing Nan's first name. I loved the idea and didn't look back.

Elizabeth – I grew up watching my now incredible friend, Liz on tv. An inspiration for my creativity since I was eight, I just had to include her gorgeous name somewhere important. As long as I have known her, Liz has shown me nothing but kindness, and shares her wisdom with me, and always makes sure I know that she believes in me.

Pinnock – The surname of my wonderful secondary school English teacher, who always encouraged me to write and helped me navigate through some extremely difficult school days. She always told me I could do anything I ever put my mind to.

The Field Where All The Flowers Grow

Maria – I named Maria after the first person outside of my family network that I ever felt safe around. My first nursery experience was dreadful, so I was moved to another one. Maria was my key worker and one of my mum's sweet friends. I adored playing with her and she never failed to cheer me up. She even made me fairy dust to put under my bed to stop the bad dreams!

Shonda – I had to give a nod to my favourite writer out there, Shonda Rhimes! A strong, powerful, and so very creative woman that inspired me to carry on writing even when things got in the way.

Elijah – I had a childhood friend named Elijah from ages 7 to 8. He moved away and we completely fell out of touch, but I always had such fun playing with him, and we used to create our own magical games. He was always the kindest.

Julie – My first favourite actress, Julie Andrews. Breath-taking, gracious, elegant, and everything I wanted this character to be.

Peter – My incredible Grandad's name. One of the reasons I had Mary be an artist was because I love looking through my grandad's artwork and hearing stories about the amazing things he has created.

"Sometimes, a door closes and the whole world opens right up." – I'm not sure if she even remembers messaging this to me, but it is my favourite piece of wisdom Liz has ever taught me. I will remember it forever.

"Being brave isn't having zero fear." – My mum always tells me that it makes me even braver to do something when I'm scared to do it. The more afraid you are, the braver you'll be.

The anaphorical reference to lavender – Almost exactly a year ago, my mum took me to a stunning lavender field. We spent the whole day together, just us and it's a memory I will cherish forever.

There are obviously, so many wonderful people in my life that I couldn't possibly name them all. I trust they know who they are and know how incredibly grateful I am to know them.

Feel free to follow my –

Instagram – felicity_jayne

Or email me at

felicityemmagraceotoole@gmail.com

Thank you so very much for reading!

Printed in Great Britain
by Amazon